THE FORTUNES OF TEXAS

*Follow the lives and loves of a complex family
with a rich history and deep ties
in the Lone Star State*

FORTUNE'S SECRET CHILDREN

*Six siblings discover they're actually part of
the notorious Fortune family and move to
Chatelaine, Texas, to claim their name...while
uncovering shocking truths and life-changing
surprises. Will their Fortunes turn—hopefully, for
the better?*

FORTUNE'S FAUX ENGAGEMENT

A chance meeting with some high-school
frenemies compels Jade Fortune to pretend
that Heath Blackwood, the most sought-after
bachelor in Chatelaine, is her fiancé! Talk about
awkward—especially when the new-in-town tech
titan is desperately seeking answers about his
own past. But to Jade's surprise, Heath's happy
to play along with her spur-of-the-moment ruse.
Maybe their fake fling could be the stuff dreams
are made of?

Dear Reader,

This was my first time writing in the world of the Fortune family. I enjoyed Heath and Jade going from a fake engagement to having genuine feelings for one another. I especially loved writing about Jade's basset hound, Charlie. If you're familiar with my other stories, you know how much I love my canine characters, and Charlie was no exception. Dressing him up in a Halloween costume was such fun. Too bad he didn't agree! I hope you enjoy reading about Charlie and his humans, Jade and Heath.

Let me know what you think. You can reach me at authorcarrienichols@gmail.com. I always love connecting with readers. And check out my website, carrienichols.com, for updates on new releases.

Thanks, and happy reading!

Carrie

FORTUNE'S FAUX ENGAGEMENT

CARRIE NICHOLS

THE FORTUNES OF TEXAS

Special thanks and acknowledgment are given to
Carrie Nichols for her contribution to
The Fortunes of Texas: Fortune's Secret Children miniseries.

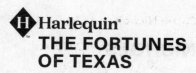

Harlequin®
THE FORTUNES
OF TEXAS

Recycling programs
for this product may
not exist in your area.

ISBN-13: 978-1-335-99674-9

Fortune's Faux Engagement

Copyright © 2024 by Harlequin Enterprises ULC

 Harlequin Enterprises ULC
22 Adelaide St. West, 41st Floor
Toronto, Ontario M5H 4E3, Canada
www.Harlequin.com

Printed in Lithuania

MIX
Paper | Supporting
responsible forestry
FSC® C021394

Carrie Nichols grew up in New England but moved south and traded snow for central AC. She loves to travel, is addicted to British crime dramas and knows a *Seinfeld* quote appropriate for every occasion.

A 2016 RWA Golden Heart® Award winner and two-time Maggie Award for Excellence winner, she has one tolerant husband, two grown sons and two critical cats. To her dismay, Carrie's characters—like her family—often ignore the wisdom and guidance she offers.

Books by Carrie Nichols

The Fortunes of Texas: Fortune's Secret Children

Fortune's Faux Engagement

Harlequin Special Edition

Small-Town Sweethearts

The Marine's Secret Daughter
The Sergeant's Unexpected Family
His Unexpected Twins
The Scrooge of Loon Lake
The Sergeant's Matchmaking Dog
The Hero Next Door
A Hero and His Dog
His Unlikely Homecoming

Visit the Author Profile page
at Harlequin.com for more titles.

With gratitude to Dan Carney for his help with the agricultural technology ideas, and to Pippa Roscoe for the memory box idea, and to Jill Ralph for the traveling carnival idea.

Chapter One

Jade Fortune's feet skidded to a stop the moment she spotted the shiny black Mercedes G Wagon. She wouldn't have been surprised if her favorite red Chuck Taylors had left skid marks on the pavement.

Heath Blackwood must be in town. Her heart began pumping faster.

It had to be him. Heath was the only one she knew in Chatelaine, Texas, who drove that particular color and model of SUV. Not only did he drive a G Wagon, but it had been showroom clean every time she'd seen it. Just like the one parked in front of the Daily Grind.

"I can barely manage dust-free for a day. And I'm not just talking about my truck," Jade muttered, glancing down at her companion, who'd been forced to stop when she did. "How do you suppose he does it?"

The answer was a short, baying bark.

She nodded. "You're right. It is a mystery."

Charlie looked up at her with his soulful basset hound eyes as if wondering why she was carrying on this particular conversation with him. Considering it didn't involve any of his favorite words—treat, walk, ride or nap—he wasn't interested.

"Sorry, but this is what happens when you're thirty-three, single and haven't had a date in ages. You end up carrying on most conversations with your dog," she told him.

He shook his head, his long ears flapping noisily. He'd also succeeded in scattering doggie drool everywhere.

"Ewww." Jade pulled a paper napkin from the front pocket of her jeans. When you owned a basset, you learned to be prepared. She swiped at her pant leg. "Drool or no, we've been together longer than any of the guys I've dated, and you've been the most loyal, so you're forgiven."

Charlie wagged his tail and gave her a cheerful bark.

"You're right, I have no business complaining. I'm in a good place in my life. I don't need a man to prove that."

After a dozen years of drifting through life and a series of dead-end jobs, she was settled. And content. Living on the Fortune family ranch and updating and expanding the petting zoo kept her busy. She also set up workshops and day camps to teach school children about animals and agriculture. Both were more rewarding and fulfilling than anything she'd ever done.

Sure, she had experts guiding her with the zoo part, but she was as hands-on as possible, even picking up a rake or shovel and cleaning up after the animals when necessary. She spent a lot of time studying so she could teach many of the offered workshops herself, depending on subject matter and the age of the students. Jade also tracked down and invited experts to come to lecture whenever possible. That approach worked best for older kids who might require more in-depth knowledge than she could provide.

Her work life might be stable, but she doubted her single status was about to change anytime soon. With Dahlia and Sabrina happily ensconced in loving relationships, her mother and, to a certain extent, her sisters were now trying their best to matchmake her. She'd gone on a couple of casual dates but wasn't likely to become serious about anyone else while she had this pesky crush on the utterly gorgeous, utterly unobtainable Heath Blackwood.

Yes, she was happy and in a good place but…

Sometimes, late at night when she couldn't sleep, the thought of Heath Blackwood's broad shoulders and deep blue eyes gave her tingles and—

"Nope. I've got to cut that out. I'm sure he doesn't even know I exist." She tossed the napkin in the trash can in front of her original destination, Longhorn's Farm & Feed.

Jingling the leash, she said, "C'mon, Charlie, let's get this poster inside the store before you slobber all over it too."

Standing in the entrance to the feed store, she allowed herself another glance across the street to the Mercedes parked in a prime spot at the coffee shop. Well, the Daily Grind was Chatelaine's version of a coffee shop. Granted, it had a barista and sold a variety of coffee concoctions along with yummy pastries just like the iconic shops in Dallas or Houston, but that's where the resemblance ended.

The shop was located in a modest bungalow that had been converted into an eatery in the 1930s and hadn't changed much since except for the wide porch that ran the length of the front of the building, which now acted as take out for coffee and pastries A few tables were scattered there for customers who preferred to sit outside to enjoy their coffee.

That parked Mercedes meant Heath Blackwood was probably in the shop. So close. She made an impatient sound with her tongue and turned away to continue into the feed store but paused in the doorway to adjust to the dimmer interior after being in the bright October sunshine.

Inside the store, Jade unrolled the poster and brought it to Phyllis Castleberry, who was manning the cash register today. Phyllis was reputed to be in her seventies, but her age was not a subject you discussed with her or with anyone else if you knew what was good for you. Same with her teased and sprayed bottle-blond helmet of hair.

"Hey, Phyllis, can I leave this with you? It's all about Halloween Happenings at the petting zoo. Starting in the middle of the month, we'll be offering hayrides, pumpkin decorating fun and a costume parade for kids and their pets."

Phyllis raised one of her pencil-enhanced eyebrows. "Pets in costumes? I gotta see that. Are you dressing Charlie up?"

"Of course. It's part of his duty as grand marshal of the parade," Jade told her and glanced at her beloved pooch, who plopped his butt onto the floor with a long-suffering sigh. Jade would swear that Charlie's canine brain understood a lot more of what was said than most people gave him credit for.

Phyllis put her arms on the counter and leaned over so she could get a look at Charlie. With her short stature, she needed the boost and to brace herself to see him on the floor. "Such a sweet thing. If a trifle slow."

Yup, that's what Jade was talking about. She glanced down at Charlie, who looked up at her with what Jade considered a dog version of an eye roll. She nodded in commiseration. If she thought it would do any good, she'd correct Phyllis, but in the short time she'd known the woman, Jade had learned nothing short of an act of God could get the older woman to change her opinion. On anything.

Best to change the subject. "So, about the poster. Can I leave one here?"

"Of course, dear." Phyllis glanced at the poster, her lips moving as she read. "Ooh, that sounds like fun. I'll be sure to bring my granddaughters on my day off. I hope you realize how much we appreciate all you're doing for the young people in town."

"Thanks," Jade said, and she did mean it. She liked Phyllis, the other woman's opinion of Charlie's intelligence notwithstanding. "We really believe in giving back to the community and—"

"It's such a shame," Phyllis interjected with a sigh.

"What is?" Jade braced her hand on the counter and stood. Had something happened that she didn't know about? News traveled at the speed of sound in Chatelaine, but Jade wasn't always paying attention.

"You." Phyllis hitched her chin toward Jade. "You're obviously so good with kids, it's too bad you don't have a few of your own. You really ought to get married and start a family."

The older woman reached under the counter and

pulled out a roll of clear tape. She lined up the edges of the poster along the top of the counter and taped the poster to the glass countertop. "You should think seriously about starting a family. You're not getting any younger, ya know. After all, the Good Lord gave us a finite number of childbearing years."

"Thanks. I'll be sure to give it some thought," Jade said, working hard to keep her voice level. Thirty-three wasn't *ancient*, she wanted to shout but didn't. And she had to admit that every so often, she swore she heard a faint ticking and feared it might be her biological clock. Too bad she—

No. She wasn't going to fall into that trap. There was nothing wrong with her or her life. She was content and fulfilled, and that was a lot more than some married people could say.

Phyllis made marriage and kids sound easy, but first Jade would have to find a guy who was interested in doing that with her. And they weren't exactly coming out of the woodwork.

"There." The other woman smoothed the tape over the poster. "I know Chatelaine isn't like the big city, but we have our share of single men. Take Heath Blackwood, for instance…"

An image of broad shoulders and smoldering sex appeal sprang forth in Jade's mind. Looks, money and success all in one package. Yeah, and for those reasons, he was on the radar for every single female within a 150-mile radius. Probably some married ones too. What sort of chance did she stand?

You can't expect to attract a man if you don't put forth some effort in your appearance.

Jade shoved her father's caustic comments back into the box she kept them in and slammed the lid shut. She had never been able to compete in the looks or elegance department with her beauty queen mother or her two younger sisters. So she'd stopped trying ages ago.

Her mother, Wendy, maintained that Casper, her father, had loved his children and only ever wanted the best for them and that's why he could be harsh. Whether that was true or not, Jade would never know now that he was gone. She tried not to dwell on the past and the regrets she had when it came to her relationship with her dad.

"Or there's always Carl Evens, the greens keeper at the country club. No, wait. Shari at GreatStore says he started dating someone. Ooh, speaking of which, I think there's a new assistant manager working there. Maybe—"

Charlie chose that moment to bark. Standing, he tugged on the leash, his nails clicking on the cement as he headed toward the exit.

Thank you, Charlie. Who says you're not the smartest dog ever? "Well, I guess we'd better get going. Thanks for your help with the poster."

"Of course, dear, anytime."

Once outside, Jade blinked against the bright sunshine and glanced across the street before she could think better of it.

The luxury SUV was still parked in front of the Daily Grind.

"That must be some sort of sign. Right?" Jade mumbled. "Quick change of plans, Charlie."

The dog woofed as if he didn't like the sound of that.

"I think I could go for a latte," she told him. He whined but fell into step beside her as they crossed the street. Latte. Yup, that's the only reason she was heading to the coffee shop. And maybe a pastry. Nothing at all to do with the man who was inside.

The walk-up window on the porch was Chatelaine's version of a drive-through.

"You wait right here." She tied Charlie to the post in the small area out front that the owner of the shop had made for dogs. There were several filled water bowls. Charlie began to snuffle as she turned away, but Jade was ready for him and handed him an emergency dog bone she kept in her purse before he could let out an embarrassing full-blown basset howl at the indignity of being left behind.

She had just reached the top step when she spotted Heath sitting at one of the tables on the porch. She quickly and, she hoped, *smoothly* did a course correction toward the walk-up window at the far end of the porch, getting in line behind several people. No sense going inside if Heath was out here, right? And besides, if she stayed outside, she could keep an eye on Charlie.

Her gaze went back to Heath. He wore a pair of black-framed glasses as he sat hunched over his open laptop. She'd never considered glasses sexy...until now.

He seemed to be absorbed in whatever was on his laptop, a coffee cup and an untouched Boston crème donut perched beside him. Maybe after getting her latte, she'd say hello and tell him about her workshops. She'd been at the table when he'd been introduced to his triplet sisters, but they hadn't spoken. She liked to think he'd been so caught up in meeting the Perry triplets that he hadn't acknowledged her. For sure she'd taken notice of him. To think he had noticed and immediately dismissed her was too depressing.

Either way, she could ask him if he'd be interested in giving a lecture to her kids at one of the ranch's day camps. She knew his tech company worked with farmers and ranchers. Yeah, that sounded like a good reason to approach him.

"Are you sure this is the right place?" a woman who'd gotten in line behind Jade asked.

"The sign said the Daily Grind," answered another woman. "That's what they told us back at the spa."

"It doesn't look like any coffee shop I've ever seen," the first one scoffed.

Jade couldn't help grinning at their conversation. She had to agree that the Daily Grind was unique, but so was Chatelaine. And that was fine with her.

"Remember, we're not in Dallas anymore," the other woman pointed out.

The line advanced, and Jade shuffled forward as the two women's conversation flowed behind her. Something about them reminded her of the snobbish girls from her high school days. Her family's money had not spared her from the castigating tongues of those girls. So, she had spent her high school years trying to blend into the background, to avoid detection. Getting noticed for any reason meant becoming a target.

But, considering she'd reached her full adult height of five foot nine by the time she'd even started high school, it hadn't been easy. Making it worse was the fact most of the boys had not yet grown to their full height, so she towered over many of them, including her twin, Nash. He eventually flew past her and now loved patting her on the head and calling her a good *little* sister to make up for those early days.

"How do people stand it? How do you live in a place with no Nordstrom? It's practically barbaric," said one of the women with a condescending snort.

Chatelaine might not be as large or upscale as Dallas or Houston, but it was now Jade's hometown, and she was proud of it. The people here had welcomed her and her family. She'd never seen her mother so excited or happy as she had been since moving here. In fact, the last time Jade had been with her mother, the woman had been positively glowing. Jade never remembered her being like that in the past. Of course, times had not always been easy during Wendy's marriage to Casper Windham, but she'd made the best of it. Yet this…this was *different*. Wendy's happiness wasn't just her putting on a good face. You couldn't fake radiant.

"Well, I'm going to blame you if this coffee is crap," one of the women griped to her companion. "Why couldn't you have waited until we got somewhere decent to feed your caffeine habit?"

That's it! She'd heard enough out of these women. Chatelaine may not have a Nordstrom, but they had damn fine coffee.

Plastering on a smile, Jade turned around. "You don't

have to worry about the coffee here, ladies. I've had coffee in Dallas and Houston, and I'd put the Daily Grind's coffee up against those bougie shops any day."

Now, standing face-to-face with the women, Jade regretted her outburst. Heat rose to her cheeks from the uncharacteristic tirade as she tried to figure out why they looked familiar. One was a blonde with hair cascading down around her shoulders, the other a brunette, her shiny hair cut in a symmetrical bob.

The blonde, dressed in a couture designer outfit, looked trim and elegant despite the warm sun and her advanced state of pregnancy. The diamonds in the rings on her left hand sparkled in the sunlight, and Jade was tempted to caution her not to blind anyone. Also dressed in a chic outfit, the brunette carried a large, brightly patterned Dolce & Gabbana tote bag.

Jade did a double take when the head of a tiny dog popped over the top of the designer bag. The red toy poodle blinked at Jade. She'd bet that dog didn't drool all over everything and silently apologized to Charlie for even thinking it. She vowed to give him an extra dog treat when they got home. "Cute dog."

The brunette patted the poodle's head but pulled her hand away when the dog began kissing her fingers. "This is Zaza."

Jade nodded, but before she could say anything more the blonde was saying, "Jade? *Jade Windham*, is that you?"

Pocket-size dog forgotten, the hair on the back of Jade's neck stood up. How did...? Oh God, it was Alexis Baker and Nina Carpenter. No wonder they looked familiar. They were her high school nemeses, but she hadn't seen them since graduation. And she could have gone happily for the rest of her life without crossing paths with them ever again. They'd been just as snobbish back then. Not to mention, they'd made Jade's life miserable with their cutting comments disguised as helpful advice if others were present and just plain mean digs if they managed to get her alone.

"I'm not surprised you ended up in the back of beyond," Nina, the brunette, said with a brittle smile.

Jade's cheeks flushed. What was wrong with her? She was a grown woman. High school was fifteen years ago, middle school over twenty. So why did she feel like she'd been thrown back into second period biology with the school's ultimate mean girls?

"Actually, it's Jade Fortune now." *Oh no.* Why did she have to say that? She didn't want to get into that and not with Alexis and Nina of all people.

Jade had, along with her brothers and sisters, changed her last name to Fortune when their mother learned she was related to the well-known Texas family. They'd done it mostly to please Wendy. And it wasn't as if Jade had been close to Casper Windham and would miss using his name.

"Oh, that's right. I heard something about all that. Y'all found out you were Fortunes. May as well take advantage of the situation, right?" Alexis tossed her long blond hair over her shoulder, ignoring the woman behind her, who sputtered when that hair slapped her in the face.

Yeah, not much had changed.

"We decided to embrace our family connection," Jade

answered, keeping her voice as even as possible. Why hadn't she minded her own business? They might not have noticed her. But, no, she had to stick up for her new home. Now she'd called attention to herself and had to suffer the consequences. Felt like high school all over again.

Remembering their snide comments about the town, she asked, "What are you both doing in Chatelaine?"

"We were invited to enjoy the spa at Fortune's Castle," Nina told her.

Jade did her best to hide her surprise. Her mother was redoing Fortune's Castle, turning her inheritance into an exclusive resort and spa. Last time she'd spoken with her, Wendy had mentioned that she'd invited Heath to stay at the hotel in one of the finished penthouse suites. She'd also invited some women to come for a day to sample the services of the spa. Too bad her mother included these two in her invitation.

"You were invited?" Jade asked and winced. Did that make her sound pathetic?

"Of course, we were on the list." Alexis said with a sniff. "Nina is a major social media influencer, so she was invited. And she asked me to come along as her guest."

"I wouldn't have wanted to come way out here by myself," Nina said with a shudder.

Jade ground her back teeth but ignored the biting comment.

"A last girls' trip before Junior is born," Alexis said and patted her stomach.

It wasn't easy, but Jade smiled and found her manners. "Looks like it won't be too long. Congratulations. A boy, you say?"

"Thanks." Alexis waved her hand, holding it so the diamond-studded engagement and wedding bands were on display. "Yes, Conrad and the whole family are thrilled to death. I'm carrying the first grandson."

"How wonderful." Jade nodded. Why had she given in to temptation and come over here? Oh yeah, in hopes of running into Heath Blackwood. And here he was, sitting right over there and could probably hear everything these catty women were saying to her. Would he agree with them? Was it her imagination, or had the place descended into silence?

"Is it true what we heard today? You're running some sort of animal thing?" Nina asked.

"A petting zoo," Jade clarified.

"Who would have thought you'd end up running a zoo of all things? But I'm sure there's a lot more to it than cleaning up animal dung all day." Nina giggled. "At least you're wearing the right footwear for the job—"

"Jade?" Candace, the barista manning the window, leaned out. "You're next. What can I get you?"

The ability to click my *heels and be home at the ranch would be nice.*

Jade managed to smile. "A Royal English Breakfast latte, please. Oh, and I'd love a Boston crème."

"Sorry. Out of those donuts. How about a double chocolate chip muffin instead."

"No, that's okay. But thanks, Candace."

Maybe if she didn't turn back around, Nina and

Alexis would leave her be and go about their own business. *And maybe pigs would fly.*

Nina snapped her fingers. "That reminds me, I assume we'll be seeing you again next weekend."

"Next weekend?" Jade racked her brain trying to figure out what they could be talking about. Her mother hadn't mentioned anything else going on at Fortune's Castle.

Alexis nodded. "Our fifteenth high school class reunion. You are planning to attend, aren't you? You can tell everyone the exciting ins and outs of running a petting zoo. I'm sure everyone will be fascinated to learn what it's like to scoop poop all day."

The two women giggled, and Jade clenched her hands. She loved her job, and they were making fun of it. "My boyfriend wasn't sure if he could get away to come with me, so I hadn't made plans yet."

Oh no. Where had that *come from?*

"You have a boyfriend?" Nina gave her a critical once over.

Jade wiped at the damp spot on her jeans from Charlie's drool. "My fiancé actually."

Oh, Jade, where is your head at? When you're in a hole you are supposed to stop digging, not get a bulldozer.

"Fiancé? Really?" Alexis giggled.

"That's him right over there," Jade said and made a vague motion with her head in the general direction of Heath's table. What were the odds that they'd know him?

"Say what? You can't mean *him.* That's Heath Blackwood," Nina squeaked.

So much for not knowing him.

Alexis *tsked* her tongue. "You couldn't possibly be engaged to someone like Heath Blackwood."

"Oh, it's not official yet or anything, but he asked me, and I said yes. So..." Had she taken leave of her senses?

Nina gave someone a saccharine sweet smile. Jade turned her head to see who she was looking at.

Heath, no longer hunched over his laptop and intent on his screen, was watching them. His forehead wrinkled in a frown. Had he overheard the conversation?

Shoot me now.

Or worse. Maybe he knew Nina and Alexis. Perhaps he was business associates or golfing partners with their husbands, and he was coming over to say hi to them. And they would rat her out.

She groaned inwardly. Why oh why had she opened her big mouth and let all those stupid lies spew forth? Maybe her dad was right. There was something seriously wrong with her.

Where were the Four Horsemen of the Apocalypse heralding the end of the world? She'd just claimed to be Heath Blackwood's fiancée. That surely was the end of *her* world. Because if anyone had overheard her, her life in Chatelaine was over. She'd be laughed out of town if anyone got wind of this.

And it would be her own damn fault.

Jade Fortune.

Heath had spotted her as soon as she came out of the feed store and crossed the street. Dressed in worn jeans, a T-shirt and red sneakers, Jade was long and lithe but round in all the right places. Seeing her made him catch his breath.

He'd been mentally kicking himself for not introducing himself since seeing her that day in the coffee shop. But he'd been caught up with meeting his sisters. Digging into his mother's past and meeting his sisters had been the reason he'd come to Chatelaine.

But not speaking to Jade that day didn't mean he hadn't noticed her so now he felt like doing a fist bump when she got in line for the takeout window. At first it appeared she'd been planning to go inside but changed her mind at the last minute to stay outside. Had she noticed him? Is that why she'd decided to line up at the window?

Ego much, Blackwood?

Maybe he should go up and actually introduce himself this time. Then they could talk. He huffed out a short laugh. This wasn't one of those Jane Austen type movies his mom had watched all the time. No need these days for a formal introduction in order to speak to her. Except the thought of talking to her made his mouth go dry. Made him feel like he was in his youth. When the girls hadn't paid any attention to the gangly, fatherless boy from the wrong side of the tracks.

But, man, they'd sure noticed once he'd achieved success with his start-up tech company and he'd shot up into the tax bracket he now occupied. Except all the females who threw themselves at him now left him cold. Probably had something to do with the fact that his success is what drew them.

He came to the decision to suck it up—hey, he was a

grown man, not a tongue-tied teen—and go over there. Damn. Now she was talking with those two women, so he stayed seated. He didn't want an audience in case he stumbled over his words. Why did Jade make him feel so awkward?

Truth was, she was the only one he was interested in talking to, so he may as well wait. From the first moment he'd laid eyes on her in town, he'd been fascinated. She could only be described as authentic. Each time he'd seen her, she'd been wearing jeans and a T-shirt or flannel, depending on the weather. Her long shiny hair had been tied back in a no-nonsense style instead of puffed out and sprayed, like so many of the socialites at the country club. Jade didn't seem interested in putting up a front, not like the two women behind her. He'd swear those two were all show and no substance.

He admired what Jade was doing for the children of the community. As a boy, he'd attended the sort of workshops she provided. They were free or very little cost, so his mom could afford it, and they satisfied his thirst for knowledge. Those workshops had also fueled his imagination, and he credited them with helping him, a fatherless boy, reach his potential, fulfill his dreams and beyond. He'd created his own innovative company to help farmers and ranchers. His first idea had made him millions. It had been a special weather forecast application useful for both farmers and ranchers.

Moving on from weather apps, he'd been researching drones and lasers, wanting to take his company in a new direction. He liked the idea of using drones, along with artificial intelligence, to target and kill invasive weeds with lasers. This was an up-and-coming technology for farmers, and he wanted in on the ground floor, dumping his profits back into research for this technology—

Hang on. Did someone just mention *his* name? Glancing around, he brought his thoughts back to the present and the coffee shop.

The blonde who was carrying a purse that looked large enough to stock a small country was staring intently at him. A tiny red curly-haired creature popped its head out of the large tote. Was that a *dog*?

The two uppity women glanced his way, and Jade was looking increasingly uncomfortable. Was something wrong? It might not be any of his business, but he decided to pay closer attention to the conversation because it was affecting Jade.

From what he could gather, the ladies were acquainted with Jade, but he'd never seen them around town until today.

He caught enough of the conversation to be angry on Jade's behalf. Running the petting zoo was not something to be denigrated. It wasn't just the kids who benefited but the entire town. In the short time he'd been part of it, he'd come to like the people who lived here.

What the...?

Intent on preventing those women from humiliating Jade, he pushed his chair back so quickly it fell over with a clatter. All three women turned at the sound.

He tossed his glasses onto the table and stalked across the porch, coming to Jade's rescue his only goal.

"Sweetheart, I've been waiting for you," he declared as he approached.

Jade's eyes widened. "Well, I—"

He threw his arms around her, cutting off what she'd been about to say and pulling her close.

Leaning down, he whispered in her ear. "Play along."

She parted her lips as if to speak but his mouth claimed hers before any words came out.

Chapter Two

It was supposed to be a quick peck on the mouth, but once his lips met hers, he couldn't move away as quickly as he planned. He savored the feel of those soft lips against his. At the beginning of the kiss, she'd held herself stiff against him, but she began to relax, her softness molding to his hardness. As if she belonged there. For a moment, he wished she did. The kiss was invigorating, like the hint of autumn that was in the air today.

"You can't be serious," one of the women sputtered and broke the spell Jade had cast over him.

He pulled his mouth away from Jade's but kept a proprietary arm around her waist. "Why not?"

"Because you're so important and…and I don't see a ring," the blonde one said with a smug expression, as if she'd caught them in a lie. She flipped her hair over her shoulder.

Well, she had caught them, but he wasn't going to turn on Jade now.

"We're getting it sized," he lied smoothly. He turned to Jade. "Sweetheart, aren't you going to introduce me to your…friends? I don't know them, although they seem to know all about me. Or think they do."

"Of course they know you. You being so important and all," Jade said with an amused grin.

Ah, she had a sense of humor. He liked that and silently saluted her. Tapping a finger to the end of her nose, he retorted, "And you didn't believe me when I tried to tell you that."

Jade laughed, and his gut tightened again, but for a very different reason this time. She had a clear, robust laugh and he loved it, wanted to hear it again. Wanted to be the one making her laugh.

Still smiling, she held her hand out toward the other two. "Heath, this is Nina Carpenter and Alexis Baker."

"Actually, it's Alexis Heede now," the blonde said with a disdainful sniff.

So not *a gracious loser*, he thought dryly. He could be all wrong, but he imagined Jade being well mannered, even in defeat.

Evidently, Alexis figured she was important enough for that information to be common knowledge. Yeah, he had made the right choice to back up Jade's lie even though he didn't condone lying.

"And I'm still Carpenter, but that's all about to change next year. That's part of why we were checking out the spa at Fortune's Castle. I'm deciding on venues for a bachelorette party. It's going to be a fabulous blowout. My fiancé said to spare no expense. He is such a dear. But I'm sure you know him, Heath. He's Trevor Trudeau of Trudeau, Fitch and Wilson."

Heath made an exaggerated grimace. "If I admit I don't know him, will that change my status as someone important?"

Jade gave him a playful slap on the arm. "You are such a tease. I'm sure he knows all about your husband, because Heath isn't just important, he knows everyone who *is* important."

Touché. Heath met Jade's gaze and silently indicated that he knew what she'd done there, because he hadn't known her two former classmates.

The barista stuck her head out the window. "I hate to break up this reunion, but your latte is ready, Jade."

Heath stepped forward and pulled out his wallet. "I've got this. You can sit at the table I saved for us, sweetheart."

"Speaking of reunion, can we expect to see *both* of you next weekend at the class reunion in Cactus Grove?" Nina asked, her smug gaze bouncing between them.

Jade shifted her feet. "Well, I...that is, we—"

"We wouldn't miss it. I'm looking forward to meeting the rest of Jade's friends," Heath said. After that kiss, he wasn't about to let Jade Fortune slip away before he had a chance to get to know her better. He'd been attracted to her since first laying eyes on her shortly after he'd arrived in town, but that intoxicating lip-lock had been a game changer. Talk about chemistry.

Jade looked up at him, her expression surprised. "You are?"

"Now who's teasing?" He gave her a quick kiss. He did it because he'd been dying for a repeat performance and wanted to see if he could recreate the zing he felt when his lips had first touched hers.

Yep, still there. Not a fluke. And it felt...*right*. More right than anything else he'd experienced with a woman.

The barista stuck her head out the window. "Are you ladies ready to order? You're holding up the line."

"Well, we'll let you place your order. Hope to see you both next weekend," Heath said and led Jade to his table. He carried her drink in one hand and placed the other on the middle of her back in a proprietary gesture. Those two women weren't the only ones whose gaze was glued to them, but he didn't care.

There was only a scattering of customers on the porch, but that's all it would take for word to get around town about him and Jade. The gossips would be linking their names together. He thought about that for a moment and realized he didn't mind being linked with Jade, a woman he admired and who inexplicitly made his pulse race.

"I can't tell you how sorry I am about all this," she was saying as she slipped into a seat at his table.

He set her drink in front of her. "Don't worry about it."

"How can I *not* worry about it? You realize these people—" she paused and glanced around "—overheard most of that. I've probably ruined your life."

He barked out a laugh, which he regretted when he saw her misery was genuine. He covered her hand with his. "You have done no such thing. If anything, you've raised my status."

"How do you figure that?"

"Being engaged to a Fortune can only help me in Chatelaine."

She quirked a brow. "Is that why you didn't tell them I made it all up?"

He had a much more specific reason for not contradicting her, but he wasn't ready to share that. Not yet anyway. So, he shrugged.

"Oh, geez." She clapped a hand over her mouth.

"What? What's the matter?"

She took her hand away from her mouth and waved it around. "I just realized. What if you are involved with someone, and they hear about this? I've probably messed—"

He grabbed her flailing hand. "There's no other woman. At least those two got something right."

"You're sure?"

"I'm positive." He squeezed her hand before releasing it.

"Thank goodness," she muttered and peeled the cover off the drink, pulled out a tea bag and squeezed it. She wore no rings, and her nails were trimmed and unadorned, but he found her hands appealing. What would they feel like on him? Would her touch be bold or tentative?

He shook his head, hoping to scatter those thoughts. She stirred the drink, mixing the foam that floated on top.

"What is that?" he asked.

"A Royal English Breakfast tea latte."

"That's a thing?"

"Like I told Alexis and Nina, the Daily Grind can hold its own with any bougie shop out there."

He grinned. "You did, didn't you?"

She heaved a sigh. "I should have kept my mouth shut. Maybe they wouldn't have even noticed me."

"I find that hard to believe." He'd noticed her from across the street.

She brought the tea to her mouth and blew on it before taking a sip. "Why would you say that?"

"You're very noticeable, Jade Fortune." His focus the last time they'd been together at the coffee shop had been on meeting his sisters for the first time but that didn't mean he hadn't noticed her even if he hadn't said anything.

She laughed and shook her head. "You say that like it's a good thing."

"Believe me, it is."

"I'll bet you're sorry I noticed you and dragged you into my mess like something straight out of a high school drama club production."

"Like I said, I was happy to come to your rescue." And he meant it. When he'd gotten up and walked over, he'd intended to just divert the women's attention, but once he opened his mouth, he'd found himself backing up her claim.

"How can you be so cavalier about this?"

He shrugged because he wasn't sure he knew the answer to that himself. He didn't want to admit he was drawn to her. Not yet anyway. "If I hadn't come to your rescue, I might never have found out how important I am. So there's that."

She laughed. Oh man, he liked that laugh.

"I would have said they were hitting on you by appealing to your ego, but they're both attached so..."

Now he laughed. "Even if they were trying to flirt with me, do you think I'd fall for it?"

"I don't know. I wouldn't have expected you to back up my outrageous claim, but you did."

He frowned. "Why is it so outrageous that we could be involved?"

"Well, because…because…" She shook her head. "We don't even know one another."

"We can change that. We have week before the re-union."

Her eyes widened. "You mean you really intend to go?"

"I told those snobs I was, so I will." And he could use that occasion as an excuse to get to know Jade Fortune. Not that he needed an excuse, but he liked to cover his bases.

Jade seemed to give it some consideration and finally nodded. He let go of the breath he'd been holding and smiled. "Good."

"So, you're the one who grabbed the last Boston crème," she said, pointing her chin at the uneaten donut on the table and sighed. "Lucky you."

She wanted the pastry, that much was clear. Did he want to just be a gentleman and give it to her or… "I'm willing to share."

"No. Honestly." She blushed. "I shouldn't have said anything."

He rose and took several steps back to the counter that held napkins and creamers and scooped up a cellophane-wrapped napkin and plastic cutlery packet. Sitting back down across from Jade at the small square table, he ripped open the packet. "There. I even have a knife to divide it."

"You're my hero," she said then blushed as if realizing what she'd said.

"That's good to know." The blush highlighted a smattering of freckles across the bridge of her nose. He hadn't noticed those before, and he shifted in his seat as he took note of them now. He'd love to take his time counting them, punctuating his exploration with kisses and the tip of his tongue.

Damn. If he didn't knock this off, he'd be blushing too. To concentrate on something other than those alluring spots, he cut the pastry in half. Some of the pastry cream filling squirted onto the plate from the donut.

"Sorry. I seem to have made a mess of this," he muttered. He should have known better than to try and divide it with such a heavy-handed movement. He should have just given the donut to her, but for some silly reason, sharing the pastry seemed more intimate than just giving her the entire thing.

"That's okay," she said and stuck a finger in the cream and brought it to her lips.

He cleared his throat and shifted in his seat, unable to take his eyes away from her mouth.

"You've got some…" he said, and before his good sense could take over, he reached out and touched a fingertip to the corner of her mouth and wiped off the spot of filling.

Her eyes widened at his touch, and he quickly drew away, bringing the finger to his own lips. Damn, what was he doing?

What was it about this woman that not only piqued his curiosity but had his imagination in overdrive?

* * *

Oh no! What in the world was she doing scraping the filling up with her fingers? Jade had no choice now but to taste the pastry cream. Talk about being obvious. She ate it then wiped her hand on the napkin.

She swallowed hard. Twice. It was either that or drool. And it certainly wasn't the pastry causing it. The donut was delicious but couldn't compete with the delectable man seated across from her. And he was watching her every move.

Maybe he was afraid of what she might say or do next. Not that she could blame him. She certainly wasn't acting like the Jade Fortune who was awkward around men.

"I'm so sorry. I don't know what made me say that we were engaged," Jade said, trying not to let her misery show on her face. She thought about that kiss. Had he done it to be kind? Pity was the absolute last thing she wanted from Heath Blackwood.

"It's okay," he replied with a negligent lift of one shoulder.

Why was he being so nice about this whole debacle? It just made her feel worse. If he'd been angry or gave her a hard time, she'd feel a whole lot better about the situation. "No, it's *not* okay. I never should have made that claim. What was I thinking? Oh, wait. I wasn't."

"Yeah, I got the feeling maybe you were just reacting to the vitriol those two were throwing at you."

"They used to bully me in school," she admitted. Oh, why had she said that? Talk about looking pathetic in front of the hottest guy in Chatelaine. Maybe she should have checked her horoscope before leaving home today. It might have warned her not to open her mouth.

"I hate dealing with bullies."

"I can't imagine you have to deal with them."

"Believe it or not, I wasn't always this important," he said with a lopsided grin.

She pressed her palm against her chest. "No! Say it isn't so."

He laughed and she joined him. It felt good to be sharing not only a pastry but a joke with a handsome man.

See, Dad, maybe I'm not such a failure after all.

"But it is true that I didn't grow into my greatness until much later. I was referred to as a shrimp well into high school," he confided.

"I had the opposite problem. I reached my full height in eighth grade."

He winced. "Ouch, you must have towered over the boys."

"That's for sure."

"I'm not sure I would have let that stop me if I'd known you in high school," Heath murmured.

"Oh, you would have. I wasn't exactly Miss Popularity."

"Don't be too sure. You have a lot of appeal."

"Those two didn't seem to think so." She hitched her chin toward Alexis and Nina, who were walking back to a white Range Rover. Unlike Heath's SUV, theirs was dusty, and Jade got some perverse pleasure out of that. That was pretty juvenile, but she couldn't help it.

"Forget about them. Tell me more about yourself."

"Not much to tell. You may find this hard to believe,

but I don't always go around claiming to be engaged to strange men."

"Wait." He drew back. "How did I go from important to *strange*?"

Her cheeks heated. "Let me rephrase that. I don't claim to be engaged to strangers."

"Then I'm honored you chose me."

"Again, I apologize. I still don't understand why you didn't tell them the truth."

"And humiliate you? No way." He looked over her shoulder for a moment as if deciding on something. "When I was in elementary school, I won a statewide science award. Some of the other boys, I'd say they were male versions of Alexis and..."

"Nina."

"Right." He paused for a moment as if deciding something. "As I was saying, they used to make fun of me because I never had a dad come to anything. I told everyone they'd get to see my father at the ceremony for that science award."

She put her hand on his arm and squeezed in sympathy. She'd had a dad, but he didn't always come to things like that. Not that she'd done anything outstanding like win a science award. "What happened?"

"Well, since I didn't have one, he obviously couldn't come. Luckily, my mother, bless her soul, saved the day and told the others that he'd been called out of town on important business. She spared me from public humiliation because those kids couldn't imagine my mother backing me up." He huffed out a breath. "But that's because they didn't know my mom."

"I'm glad it worked out."

He shrugged. "It did and it didn't."

"How so?"

"She saved me but, in the process, I hurt her. Even though we didn't talk about it much, I knew she felt guilty because I didn't have a father. And I'm sure she knew I always longed for one, especially when I saw the other boys with their dads. Playing ball, going fishing, stuff like that. So, with my lies I piled on more guilt. That was my bad." He looked straight ahead, but his gaze was unfocused, as if he were lost in the past.

"You were a kid. I'm sure she took that into consideration. On the other hand, I don't have that as an excuse. I'm an adult and should have handled that whole situation better. Again, I'm truly sorry I dragged you into it."

"Those girls were giving you grief you don't deserve. I think what you're doing for the kids and this town is terrific."

She swallowed. "You do?"

A tingle ran down her spine. Heath Blackwood knew about her camps and classes. Talk about catching her off guard!

"Why are you so surprised?"

"It's just that I drifted for a long time, but this feels right. Yet at the same time, I sometimes wonder if my family felt sorry and just gave me something to do. Patted me on the head and said, 'Sure, make a zoo.'"

"It's not just the zoo but those workshops you're doing. They meant so much to me as a kid."

"Really?" Maybe she wasn't just wasting her family's time, space and money with her zoo and activities on the ranch after all.

"Yes, really." He grinned. "I went to a lot of them as a kid. Where do you think I got the idea for my start-up company? I used to daydream about the stuff I learned and about making it better."

"Well, you've been very successful. Would you be willing to come and talk to the kids sometime? Let them know a little bit about what you're doing." *Please say you'll come.*

His smile lit up his blue eyes, and they resembled the sky on a sunny day. "I thought you'd never ask."

"I... I would have asked earlier, but I wasn't sure if you'd be interested. I know how busy you are."

"Not too busy to help the next generation of innovators."

"I can't thank you enough. First for pulling my butt out of the fire and now this. How will I ever repay you?"

"Have dinner with me?"

Her heart skipped a beat. "You want to have dinner with me?" She'd imagined this scenario ever since she'd realized she had a crush on him, but those had been pipe dreams. This was *real*.

"Yes, that's why I'm asking."

"But...but..."

"Why wouldn't I want to have dinner with you?"

Yeah, why? She might not be able to compete with her mother and sisters in the glamour department, but she was honest enough to know she was attractive. And fishing for compliments was beneath her. But this whole situation had her flummoxed. "Well, because—"

He tsked. "Jade, don't tell me you let those women get inside your head."

"I wasn't going to let them, but then it was like I was back in high school and feeling all awkward. How could I have let them do that to me? And to involve you was unforgivable."

"It's easy to get sucked back into situations from the past. And I involved myself. I could have denied even knowing you, but as I mentioned before, I know what it's like to be bullied." He winked at her. "And what matters now is that you're giving back and helping kids. What are those women doing to help shape the future?"

"Nina is an important social media influencer."

"I rest my case." He laughed.

Glancing at his watch, he scowled. "Unfortunately, I have to get back. I have a video meeting with my research and development team this afternoon."

"Okay."

"About tonight…"

Jade kept her smile in place. He was probably coming to his senses and going to cancel. "It's—"

He pulled out his phone. "Give me your number and I'll program it in and text you so we'll have each other's numbers. But if you don't hear from me, I'll pick you up at seven."

"Uh, do you know where I live?" she asked.

A spot of color appeared high on his cheeks. "Yeah, I guess that would help."

She gave him her address and he typed it into his phone.

After doing that, Heath leaned down and gave her a peck on the cheek. "Until tonight."

Jade sighed, admiring Heath's confident, loose-limbed stride as rushed down the steps of the coffee shop. Did all of that just happen?

She brought her fingers to her cheek, touching where his lips had been.

On his way out, Heath passed a couple with a baby coming up the steps as he was going down, but she only had eyes for him. She stood up to clear off the table before she left.

"Jade?"

She glanced at the couple on the porch and quickly revised her original assessment. The man was her brother Ridge. He and the woman with him, Hope, weren't a real couple.

As far as Jade knew, Ridge had found Hope passed out in his barn back in July. No one knew if Hope was even her real name because she claimed to have amnesia.

No, wait. Using the word *claimed* wasn't fair. Jade truly believed Hope was telling the truth about her lack of memory. Jade had come to know the mysterious woman in the past three months and didn't believe her capable of deception. She was definitely a good mother and took excellent care of baby Evie.

But that didn't prevent Jade from worrying about her brother. She could see how much he was starting to care of Hope and the baby. Given their matching tiny birthmarks and how much the baby resembled her, it seemed obvious that Hope was the infant's mother.

What if Hope recovered her memory and discovered she was a married woman? A husband and family could be searching for her at this very moment. Jade hated to think of Ridge falling for Hope and the baby only to be heartbroken when the truth was discovered. And the truth *would* eventually come out. She couldn't imagine a woman and child going missing forever and no one noticing.

"I thought that was Charlie tied up out there." Ridge came over and gave Jade a brotherly one-armed hug. "Evie recognized him too. She started cooing and kicking her feet."

Jade hugged Hope and kissed the top of baby Evie's head. She couldn't help but fall in love with the sunny, smiling baby. Maybe someday she'd—

"Was that Heath Blackwood with you? What were you two doing together?" Ridge gave her an assessing look.

"We...uh, we were just chatting. He's interested in giving a workshop for my kids sometime." And that was the truth. Or *part* of it.

"Well, rumor has it he was kissing you."

"Oh...um, that." Heat rose in her face. She should have known that little incident wouldn't go unnoticed.

"Maybe your sister would like her privacy," Hope suggested gently.

Ridge huffed out a short laugh. "Then they shouldn't have been kissing in public. Jade?"

Great. She was going to have to confess. The whole of Chatelaine would probably know about all this by tonight anyway, so what did it matter? How the heck could she have gotten herself into such hot water? She'd love to place the blame on Alexis and Nina, but she was the one who'd opened her mouth.

"Would you mind going ahead and ordering for us?" Hope asked him. "I would love a Boston crème."

Ridge glanced between the two women. "Fine, but I expect a full explanation when I get back."

It was a reprieve at least. Time to get her thoughts together. Maybe find a way to tell them what had happened without making herself look foolish. Yeah, right. "A word of warning. Those donuts are all gone. Heath and I shared the last one."

Ridge raised his eyebrows at her. "You two split a pastry?"

Why, oh, why, hadn't she kept her mouth shut?

Hope touched Ridge's shoulder. "I'll have an eclair with my latte. Can you hurry before they're all gone too?"

Ridge grumbled but went to the walk-up window.

"Thank you," Jade told Hope as her brother strode away.

Hope laughed and sat down, settling Evie on her lap. The baby was drooling and gumming a teething ring. "Don't thank me yet, I'm just as curious as he is. After all, this is Heath Blackwood we're talking about."

"You'll get the whole sordid tale. I promise." Jade sat down in the chair she'd recently vacated.

"Ooh, this is sounding better and better," Hope said, rubbing Evie's back in soothing circles.

"While we wait, why don't you tell me how you've been? I've been thinking about you. Are you still having those dreams?" Jade asked, although they sounded more like nightmares.

Hope had told her about her dreams of a middle-aged

couple holding their arms out to her and the baby, but when Hope doesn't turn over the baby, their faces become mean.

A woman came out of the coffee shop with a giggling child darting ahead carrying a pastry box. "Give me that," the woman called in an exasperated tone.

Hope's face drained of all color. Jade reached over and placed her hand over her friend's. "Hope, what is it? What's wrong?"

"I don't know." She began to shiver and wrapped her arms around Evie and clung to her. "I want to go home. Now."

Evie started to fuss and squirm, and Hope kissed the top of the baby's head, rubbing her cheek against the baby's fine hair. "Shh, sweetie, it's okay. I won't let anything happen to you."

Now it was Jade's turn to shiver. She couldn't imagine what horrific event put that much fear into Hope. Whatever happened was bad enough that she'd blocked it out, and it was giving her nightmares and panic attacks.

"Nothing is going to happen to either of you," Jade promised, trying to comfort her friend. "What do you want me to do?"

Hope gnawed on her lower lip. "Tell Ridge that Evie and I need to go home. Right now."

Jade nodded, wondering where Hope meant when she said "home." Had the other woman regained her memory? Did she want Ridge to take her home, as in where she came from? Or did Hope consider the Fortune family ranch to be home?

The baby continued to fuss. Probably picking up on her mother's stress. And Hope was certainly stressed.

Her face had drained of color, and her gaze darted about as if she expected something to happen.

Jade was torn between soothing mother and baby and getting her brother's attention as quickly as possible. She could have stayed with Hope and yelled across the porch to him, but she figured that hot kiss had caused enough of a spectacle in the Daily Grind to keep the gossip flying around Chatelaine for the foreseeable future.

Chapter Three

Rising from her chair, Jade touched Hope's shoulder in a reassuring gesture that mirrored the loving pats Hope was giving the baby. As worried as Jade was about Ridge getting hurt because of his deepening tenderness toward Hope and baby Evie, she herself was developing feelings for them too.

As much as Jade wanted to, up to now, she'd refrained from giving Ridge any unsolicited advice. She knew how it felt to have her family all up in her business, and she was sure they would be all over this whole fake engagement thing.

"Ridge, Hope wants to go home." Jade told him.

Jade patted Evie. "I have to get home, too. Got lots to do."

"Got a big date planned, Sis?" Ridge joked.

For once she could answer in the affirmative. At least she guessed it was a date. Heath was taking her to dinner, so of course it was a date. Wasn't it? Or were they as fake as the engagement?

"Sis?"

"Well, I…"

"You do." Ridge peered at her, then glanced over to

where Heath's Mercedes had been parked. "With Heath Blackwood?"

The questions and speculation had already started, and Ridge didn't even know about the fake engagement, just tonight's date. "Look, you better get Hope home. We'll talk later."

"We definitely will," Ridge promised.

Yeah, she had a lot of explaining to do. Maybe her family hadn't heard about what happened in the coffee shop today.

Nope, that's not a likely scenario. The whole town probably knew about it by now. At least Heath had backed her up, saving her from public humiliation.

Grinning, she went to fetch Charlie and go home to get ready.

She'd barely gotten the basset settled into his special car seat in the dusty pickup she used for ranch business when her phone started buzzing with calls and incoming texts. She checked Charlie's harness and pulled out the phone from the pocket of her jeans. Most of the messages were from her family, asking about a rumor going around town about her and Heath Blackwood.

Despite the barrage of messages, she grinned all the way home. She had a date! An honest-to-goodness date. When was the last time that had happened? And that date was with the gorgeous Heath Blackwood. Simply saying his name under her breath sent a tingle down her spine. As if that wasn't good enough, it was October but still warm enough to wear the dress her mother had insisted Jade buy for the annual Ranchers' Reception at the LC Club this summer. She could bring a shawl or shrug with her in case the evening turned cool. If she couldn't find something in her closet, she could ask one of her sisters. One of them would certainly have something appropriate... Yeah, she had a bit of explaining to do. Why, oh why, had she opened her big mouth and spouted off all that nonsense about being engaged to the gorgeous newcomer? If she was going to be thrown back into adolescent behavior, why couldn't she have invented a boyfriend who conveniently lived in Canada?

That was something a kid in middle school would do, but she'd acted like one, so why not?

Jade pressed the remote for the gate to the driveway of her home. Each one of the six log homes she and her siblings occupied had its own entry gate. She wasn't sure what the purpose was for the gates, but they were there when they moved in.

She groaned. The gates certainly didn't serve to keep people out because she spotted three golf carts lined up in front of her home. She hadn't expected the in-person third degree from her family to start quite so soon.

"They didn't even give us a chance to get home," she said to Charlie as she passed the carts so she could pull her truck closer to the house.

One of the carts was decorated with large dahlia flower decals, so she assumed her sister Dahlia was among the visitors. She'd bet the other two were her mother and sister Sabrina.

"I should have known this whole fiasco wouldn't stay a secret for long," she moaned as she pulled into the driveway.

As she always did when arriving home, Jade took a moment to thank her mother for buying the 3,500-acre ranch that she and her siblings now lived on. In addition to the ranch home and offices, the place had six magnificent log homes surrounding the shore of one side of Lake Chatelaine.

When Wendy had first discussed purchasing the ranch and invited all her children to move to what she was calling the Fortune Family Ranch, she'd said there were log cabins available for each of her children. Jade soon discovered that "log cabin" was a bit of a misnomer. Yes, they'd been constructed using logs, but they were large and luxurious, well beyond the realm of cabins. More like the ones she'd seen featured in slick magazines about those exclusive ski resort communities in Colorado.

Jade had felt guilty at first, as if her family was handing her charity by giving her the home, but when all her siblings moved into their respective log homes, she decided her guilt was misguided.

Charlie perked up and wagged his tail and began barking. The one Jade called his happy bark. She followed to where the dog was looking. Sure enough, her mother and two sisters were seated on her porch.

"Nothing like being obvious about butting into my business," she muttered to Charlie, who barked a response. When the siblings moved onto the ranch, it was understood that everyone would be afforded their privacy. The log homes had been built far enough apart to give the illusion of being alone in the Texas countryside.

Jade parked her battered ranch pickup at the end of the driveway and got out. She went to the passenger side and opened the door, unhooked the dog's harness and hefted all sixty-five pounds of him out of the seat.

"You need to grow longer legs or lose a few pounds," she told him with a grunt as she set him on the ground.

He went running over to the porch to greet his visitors as fast as those short legs would carry him. Jade's mom and sisters greeted him, showering him with affection and, Jade suspected, dog treats. Dahlia was the only one who owned a dog, an Australian cattle dog named Tripp, but they all carried dog biscuits, and Charlie knew it.

"Hey, to what do I owe the honor?" Jade asked as she approached the porch that wrapped along the length of the house. As if she didn't already know the reason for the welcoming committee.

"We just wanted to chat," Wendy said with a cheerful smile.

Her mother was doing her best to look and sound like this was some innocent visit. And failing *miserably*, because they all knew this was a mission. A mission to find out the truth about what they'd heard. And, considering how rampant gossip in Chatelaine was, there was no telling what they'd been told. The truth, fantasy or something in between. Jade voted for in between. She may not have been in Chatelaine for very long, but she had lived here long enough to know the gossip was like that old game of telephone. As the story got passed along, each person added their own spin on it so that it grew with each retelling.

"You know you could have gone inside," Jade told them and hopped up the two steps to the porch.

"We may all live on the same ranch, but we didn't

want to barge in and invade your home." Wendy rose and gave her daughter a quick hug. "We respect your right to privacy, dear."

Jade returned the embrace and laughed. "And yet I suspect you're all here to do exactly that. Invade my privacy."

"Oh, no, don't say that." Wendy frowned. "We just—"

"Jade's right," Dahlia interjected and stood. "Come clean, Mom. We're all here to find out the truth about Jade's supposed engagement with Heath Blackwood."

"'Supposed'? You make it sound as if that's impossible," Jade said, feeling defensive. The fact that she would have thought so too before the incident at the coffee shop didn't stop her from being annoyed. They were right, but it still sounded a bit insulting.

Of course, that meant she and Heath needed to play this out. If they didn't attend the reunion, everyone would assume the engagement was fake. Alexis and Nina would be sure to spread the word to her former classmates. So backing out of this whole thing wasn't feasible.

"Not impossible at all, dear, except you never once mentioned him, and I don't believe you two are acquainted enough to get engaged. If it's true, you've done an excellent job of keeping your relationship a secret."

"How did you even hear about any of this?"

"The barista is one of Miriam Stemple's granddaughters, and she told her mother, who told Miriam."

"And Miriam is…?" Yep, the game of telephone.

"We go to the same beauty salon and—"

"Never mind, I get it." Jade heaved a sigh and opened

her front door. "Might as well come in so I can explain what's going on."

Her mother and sisters trooped into the house, along with Charlie, who went from one guest to the other, greeting them and checking to see if anyone had any handouts.

"Hey, I saw that," Jade said and pointed at Dahlia. Her sister had taken a dog biscuit out of her pocket for Charlie. "I was just telling him he needed to cut back."

"But who can resist that face?"

"Evidently nobody which would explain why he gets excited anytime y'all come to visit."

"Oh, here. I almost forgot." Wendy paused to pick up the insulated soft-sided cooler she'd left on the floor next to her chair on the porch.

Jade took the package. "What is it?"

"Lasagna. I was in a mood today and made way too much."

"In a mood? Before or after you found out about my fake engagement?"

Wendy gave her a smile and a pat on the arm. "Does it matter?"

"I suppose not." But Jade knew the answer. "Feels like there's a lot here. I live alone, Mom."

"I know you do, dear, but you can divide it into smaller portions if you want and freeze it. Or—" Wendy paused as if for effect "—you could invite someone to share it with you."

"And would that someone go by the name of Heath Blackwood, hmm?"

All three women grinned at Jade. Now that her two younger sisters were happily attached, Jade knew her mother would be wanting that for her. Heck, she wanted that too. But claiming a fake engagement probably wasn't the best way to go about that.

They followed Jade into the spacious open kitchen of the log home and gathered on stools along one side of the long granite-topped island. She put the lasagna in the refrigerator and removed the gallon jug of apple cider. She set the cider and cups on the island along with a box of cinnamon sugar donut holes she'd splurged on. At least she wouldn't be tempted to eat the entire box.

After Jade got through telling them what had happened at the coffee shop, Wendy shook her head slowly and said, "I never liked those two girls."

"Yeah," Dahlia agreed, wiping her hands on a napkin. "I remember them from school. They wouldn't have anything to do with underclass students."

"That was so nice of Heath to come to your rescue and back you up," Wendy said.

"Well, I…" Jade started but Sabrina jumped in.

"Why should Jade feel grateful? Maybe Heath Blackwood is the one who should be thanking his lucky stars that the beautiful and talented Jade Fortune picked *him* to be her fake fiancé. I'm sure there were plenty of other guys in the coffee shop," Sabrina said.

"I doubt if there were plenty, but Sabrina's right, Mom," Dahlia put in.

Sabrina glanced over at her sister. "Of course I am."

Wendy looked startled for a moment, then smiled. "Yes. You're absolutely right."

Jade glanced at the women in her family and was appreciative of the support. She blinked back tears. As annoying as they could sometimes be, Jade was grateful for her family. Apart from her father, they'd always had her back, even when she was stumbling along trying to find her place in the world.

"Thanks. But Mom is sort of right. I really put my foot in my mouth with that claim," Jade said. "I was lucky Heath didn't leave me stranded and humiliated in front of those two."

Sabrina shook her head. "But he didn't. He stood up for you, and he's even agreed to go to the reunion, hasn't he?"

"How did you know that he agreed to attend my reunion?" Jade asked, narrowing her eyes.

Her sisters laughed. "Have you forgotten this is Chatelaine? The customers of the Daily Grind were given a play-by-play, and every last one of them couldn't wait to spread every juicy tidbit."

"So, my original point still stands. He wouldn't have done any of that if he didn't like you," Wendy said with a smile at her oldest daughter. "Sounds like he may like you a lot."

"And why shouldn't he? What's *not* to like?" Sabrina and Dahlia asked at the same time.

She quickly steered the conversation onto other topics, but after her mother and sisters left, Jade contemplated what they'd said. Was it possible Heath liked her as much as they seemed to think?

Heath parked his SUV in the lot of Fortune's Castle, the rambling mansion Wendy Fortune had inherited from her grandfather Wendell when he died. He gazed up at the structure as he exited his SUV. Fortune's Castle was aptly named because it was a replica of a medieval castle complete with ornate pointed arches, flying buttresses, gargoyles, and stained-glass windows. The result was odd while at the same time strangely impressive. It was something you'd expect to find in France or Germany, not Texas.

He certainly hadn't expected anything like it when he'd come to this dusty little town to make contact with his sisters. His mother's death had prompted him to begin his search in earnest for his biological father. Although he was still trying to fit the pieces of the puzzle that were his background. Why had he been separated from his sisters? Why had his mother chosen to leave Chatelaine?

His cell phone buzzed as he made his way across the parking lot to the cobblestone pathway that lead to the entrance. The phone screen identified the caller as his sister Lily, who, with her marriage to Asa Fortune, was also a member of that elite family. Chatelaine might be small, but it felt as though it were crawling with Fortunes.

"What's this I hear about you and Jade Fortune being engaged?" Lily asked before he could even say hello.

"Good afternoon to you too." He should have known word of what happened at the Daily Grind would spread through Chatelaine at the speed of sound.

"Sorry." She sighed into the phone. "It's just that we've been going crazy wondering what this sudden engagement was all about."

Now that he had found his half sisters and made contact with them, he would have to get used to having others taking an interest in his personal life. "'We'? You mean as in you and Asa?"

His sister was gloriously happy with her marriage to Asa after a bit of a rough start. He didn't know the whole story, but he did know her marriage had started as a marriage of convenience, like something from one of those romance novels his mother loved. But according to both his sister and Asa, it was now a real marriage and both couldn't be happier about it. And Heath was thrilled for them both.

"I mean 'we' as in me, Tabitha and Haley," she clarified. "I have a feeling Asa will tell me to mind my own business."

Heath grinned even though he knew his sister couldn't see him. "Smart man."

"Hey, I resent that," Lily shot back.

Heath winced. Damn, he was still navigating this whole brother and sister thing. He was grateful he'd found his half sisters and even more so that they were able to start forming a bond despite having three decades lapse before they met. "Look, I'm sorry. I didn't mean to—"

"Hey! I was just teasing. I'm told it's something siblings do a lot of. I'm just as new at this as you. We may not know exactly what happened thirty years ago, but now that we've all found one another, I thought we were going to be real siblings."

"And by 'real siblings,' I take it you mean teasing and getting into one another's business?"

"Well, yeah. I think it's a requirement or something."

She paused and sighed again. "And to be honest, Heath, it's because we care about you. You're our big brother."

According to his research, he was two months older than his triplet sisters. *Half sisters*, he amended, then regretted the amendment. They might not have shared the same mother or even grew up together, but the bond they were now forming was as strong as if they had.

"Thanks for the concern, and I apologize for the remark about getting in my business."

"Apology accepted, but that doesn't let you off the hook. I was appointed spokesperson," Lily informed him. "I'm supposed to find out what the heck is going on and report back."

"In other words, you drew the short straw."

She laughed but didn't give him an answer, and he wasn't going to press.

Heath sighed. He should have known this was coming. But frankly, he was still getting used to having sisters, to having any extended family. With his mom gone, there wasn't anyone to take an interest in his personal life. So he decided to go with the truth. "It's just a cover story."

"Cover story? Cover for *what*?"

He tried to think of a way to explain the situation so that no one thought poorly of Jade. Because he hated to think his sisters might blame her for taking advantage of a situation. "Jade got a bit carried away when confronted with some nasty women she'd gone to school with and claimed we were engaged."

"And you simply went along with it?" Lily asked, sounding skeptical.

He leaned against the G Wagon and crossed his feet at the ankles. "It was entirely my choice to back her up."

"Oh?"

It was just as he'd feared. He tried again to explain without having to get into the whole background of what prompted him to go along with Jade's assertion. "Would you rather I denied it and humiliated her in the Daily Grind?"

"Well, no. I can't claim to be close friends with her or anything, but I do like Jade."

"So do I," Heath admitted gruffly.

"Oh?" This time, Lily made that one-word sound totally different. Gone was the skepticism to be replaced with curiosity.

"Yeah," he said with a hint of a challenge in his voice. "I like Jade."

"And there's absolutely nothing wrong with that unless…"

"Unless what?"

"You don't have a wife stashed away somewhere, do you?" Lily asked.

"Nope. Not even a girlfriend or sometime girlfriend." The last woman he'd dated had dumped him when a better prospect had come along. She'd hinted around about marriage, but he hadn't taken her up on it. Yet he hadn't even dated Jade Fortune, and he'd jumped in to lay claim as her fiancé. What did that say about his feelings toward a woman he barely knew?

"But why did she claim you two were engaged?"

Heath explained the confrontation with those two snotty women at the coffee shop.

"Well, I'm proud to call you brother, Brother," Lily said after he'd finished his explanation.

Warmth filled his chest. He quite liked being a big brother. If only he could figure out why his mother had never told him about his biological father or that he even had half sisters. What was so wrong that she'd left town and never told James Perry he had a son?

Later that evening, Jade did a pirouette in front of the full-length mirror in the dressing area of the master bedroom, letting the fabric swirl around her thighs. The black dress, which ended at her knees, had bright gold and orange flowers tossed across the full skirt and a round neck with extended shoulders and front princess seams.

She didn't wear dresses very often, but she had to admit this one was flattering, even with her less than generous curves. And her mother and two older sisters wouldn't be there to outshine her, so it was all good.

Jade frowned at her reflection. "That was uncalled for," she told herself firmly.

It wasn't as if her closest female relatives went out of their way to make her look like the frumpy wallflower that she was. Her mother had been a beauty pageant winner in her younger days and was still a gloriously attractive woman. And the fact was that both of her sisters took after their mother in the glamorous looks department.

She shook her head. No time for a pity party, because she had a date with Heath Blackwood. The thought made her giddy and she laughed at her reflection. If this was a dream, she never wanted to wake up.

A knocking sound sent her rushing into the hallway and toward the front door. Several feet before she reached it, she slowed down. *Eager much, Jade?*

She inhaled deeply, trying to center herself. She could see the silhouette of Heath's broad shoulders through the inset frosted and beveled glass of the red painted door. Smoothing her dress, she smiled and threw open the door. "Welcome."

"Hi," Heath said and handed her a bouquet of sunflowers.

The paper wrapped around the flowers crinkled as she accepted the gift. She couldn't resist sticking her nose in the circle of blossoms. The subtle fragrance was natural and irresistible, whisking her back to her childhood. "Oh, thank you. I love these."

"I wasn't sure what to get, and those looked…uh…as good as any," he said, a faint blush high on his cheeks.

"I think sunflowers look happy. How can you not smile when you see them?" And how could she resist smiling at him. Tonight, he wore a light blue Oxford style shirt, black dress slacks, and shiny black Cole Haan pinch tassel loafers.

He slipped his index finger under his shirt collar. "Yeah, I guess I was thinking that too."

"Is that what you were going to say? It's okay to admit that they made you smile," she teased.

He chuckled. "Are you sure someone won't come and demand my man card?"

The delicious sound of his deep chuckle sent tingles down her spine. "We just won't answer the door if they do. Problem solved. Let me put these in some water before they wilt. C'mon in."

"Nice place you have here." He stepped inside and glanced around at the expansive living room with its soaring ceiling.

"It sorta comes with the job or the family, depending how you look at it. Another reason this ranch is perfect for us. It's not a bad perk, and each one of us has a mini mansion cabin like this."

"It is impressive. I love your fireplace."

She turned toward the two-story fieldstone wood-burning fireplace set between two soaring windows that went from floor to ceiling. "I love it too. I just wish I had more opportunities to use it. If the cabin was in someplace like Montana or Wyoming, it would come in handy a lot more."

"That's true, but then you wouldn't be here in Texas, and we wouldn't have met."

She didn't have a regular flower vase—when was the last time she'd gotten flowers?—so she filled a decorative antique pitcher with water. "And you wouldn't be forced to explain a fake engagement to your family."

Heath grinned. "A small price to pay, and my sisters seem to think it's all very romantic."

"Sounds like my sisters." She set the pitcher with the flowers on the mantel.

He walked over to her floor-to-ceiling windows. "This home is perfectly situated to capture the views of the lake."

"Yes, I know I can't complain. I'm really lucky. When my mother first bought this ranch, I was skeptical, but now I think it's the best thing she did."

"Do you like living so close to family?"

"Yes, and we're not so close that we trip over one another. If Mom had her way, we'd get together as a family to share a meal once a week," she said and tried to interpret the look that came over his face at her comment. But the expression disappeared almost as soon as it had appeared. If she hadn't been looking closely, she would have missed it. Did it have to do with Heath not growing up with his sisters? But, from what she understood, the Perry triplets didn't grow up together either.

"Yeah, thirty-five hundred acres gives humans and animals plenty of space to spread out," he said and smiled when she gave him a quizzical look. "I've spoken with your brother about using some of my company's technology for the ranch."

"That's right. I forget your technological advances have real-world applications." And that he was just as rich or more so than the Fortunes. And Casper Windham. Was Heath like her father? More interested in business and money than family or the people around him? She didn't think so, but then, she had to believe Casper had courted Wendy at some point. Why else would she have married him?

Heath glanced at his watch and she got the hint. "I need to let Charlie in before we leave. He has a secure and fenced area, but I don't like to leave him outside while I'm gone," she said, moving to open the side door.

Charlie came bounding inside. Probably knew they had a visitor and was hoping to get some more treats.

Her smile turned into a frown as he rushed past her,

because the parts of him that were supposed to be white weren't. He was covered in some sort of brown grime.

"Charlie! What in the world did you get into?"

"Is there a problem?" Heath asked from somewhere behind her.

Charlie perked up at the sound of a new voice. Her pet loved meeting new people. Well, more like he loved meeting potential victims for his mooching. Each new person he met might fall for his "she's starving me" act.

Afraid of what was coming next, Jade made a grab for him, but Charlie slipped through her arms like a greased pig. But not before he'd transferred whatever muck he'd rolled in onto her dress.

The dog made a beeline for Heath, who was standing only a few feet away.

"Watch out," Jade yelled but it was too late.

Before Heath could move out of the way, Charlie had his muddy front paws on Heath's formerly cleaned and pressed slim fit chinos.

Jade closed her eyes as if that could block out the disaster. So much for her fairy-tale night. Her dress was a mess and she was sure once she dared open her eyes, Heath's pants would be in a similar state as well.

"Well, hello, there. You must be Charlie," Heath was saying.

Even though he was being a good sport, Jade's heart sank just the same. First, she ambushed him in the coffee shop by announcing their nonexistent engagement, and now her dog was getting mud all over him. She wouldn't blame him at all if he left and wanted nothing more to do with her.

"Heath, I'm so sorry."

"Don't worry about it." He continued to rub Charlie's head and around his ears, sending her dog into a state of ecstasy. While the fastest way to her dog's heart was food, lavish praise and attention ran a close second. "It'll all come out in the wash. Fortune's Castle has a good laundry service."

Jade was confused at first but remembered that's where Heath had been staying. The luxury hotel wasn't officially open yet, but the rooms on the top floor—the luxury penthouse suites—were completed. Wendy had told Jade that Heath had approached her and asked if he could stay in one of those suites during his time in Chatelaine. He'd said he didn't mind the ongoing construction on the lower floors, and her mom had agreed, letting him stay at a reduced rate. She informed Jade that it gave her staff someone to "practice" on.

"I'll be sure my mother sends me the bill," Jade told him.

He dismissed it with a wave of the hand. "Not necessary."

"I don't know how you can act so casual. He's ruined our evening."

"I highly doubt that was his intention, and the evening's outcome has yet to be determined."

Either Heath Blackwood was the mellowest guy she'd ever met, or maybe the evening didn't mean as much to him as it meant to her. Had she been reading more than warranted into tonight? She blinked rapidly, hoping to prevent the tears that threatened to break free.

Chapter Four

Heath panicked when he saw how distressed Jade was. He was not good with emotional females. And the thought of having to witness Jade so upset was more than he could take.

"Hey, hey," Heath said and patted her back awkwardly. Despite the polished exterior he'd worked hard to pull around him like a cloak, deep down he still felt like that nerd he was in high school. Maybe that was another reason he'd jumped to Jade's rescue and why he was attracted to her. She wasn't artificial and slick like those two women today, like many of the women who vied for his attention. Even before his success with Blackwood AgriTech, women had shown interest. He wasn't vain, but he knew the face he saw in the mirror every day was attractive to women. But they were drawn to him until they realized he was just a computer gadget geek in a nice package. Many then lost interest.

Sure, when he'd made his first million, he'd dated women like Alexis and Nina like it was a rite of passage or something. But the truth was, they'd left him cold. He'd take Jade's down-to-earth personality any day. Still…

What had he gotten himself into? Maybe he should have denied her claim about the engagement back there at the Daily Grind. He'd let his crush on Jade overcome his common sense. He hadn't simply backed Jade up on her claim of an engagement with him, but he'd taken it one step further and agreed to attend the reunion. When those catty women had asked if they were attending, he could have ended it then and there by saying no. But he hadn't. Why? Because after that kiss, his thinking was muddled, and he'd agreed to attend.

Jade sucked in a quavering breath. "How can you be so calm?"

The dog plopped down in front of him and looked up, his soulful canine eyes seeming to beg for forgiveness.

Heath reached down and patted the dog on the head again. "It's okay. You didn't mean to ruin anything, did you boy?"

"How can you say that? Look at us." She pointed first at her muddy dress and then his dirt covered pants. She sighed. "I'll bet Zaza doesn't roll around in the mud."

"Zaza? Who—"

"Nina's dog."

"Ah, the red one in the tote bag." He had nothing against small dogs in general or that dog in particular, but like Jade, he preferred Charlie.

"That's the one." She nodded and frowned. "I'll bet he doesn't get covered in mud or drool all over everything."

"I'd take Charlie over him any day," Heath said because he didn't want Jade to cry or to call a halt to the evening. Both would be disastrous. "Charlie seems like a robust dog."

Robust? Now you're just babbling, Blackwood.

"That he is." She winced. "But he can also be stubborn and disobedient as you can see."

Heath laughed despite the turn the evening had taken. They wouldn't be making their dinner reservations at the LC Club, but maybe that was a good thing. Playing out this fake engagement in public might not be the smartest move. He genuinely liked Jade and didn't want her to have to face too much public scrutiny when the fake engagement ended.

He had to remember that the number one priority in his personal life right now was solving the mystery surrounding his birth and his biological father. That had to come first.

Jade was watching him, and he realized he'd lost the thread of the conversation. What had they been talking about? Yeah, the dog and the insipid comment he'd made about Charlie being robust. "I meant he's not afraid to roll in the mud, get dirty."

"If those are the guidelines, then, yeah, I suppose Charlie is the most robust dog in Chatelaine. He's not afraid to get dirty, and he's not afraid to spread the love. As evidenced by tonight's episode."

At least this silly conversation had gotten her mind off what had happened. Her melancholy seemed to have lifted. "See, now you can't say that about that other dog. Don't get me wrong, he looked nice enough, but I'll bet Charlie is more authentic. Like you."

She narrowed her eyes. "Are you comparing me to my *dog*?"

That's exactly what he'd done, but he didn't think

she'd appreciate it if he said so. Damn. He needed to salvage this. He wasn't the smoothest operator when it came to women, but most females overlooked that because of his bank balance. Except Jade didn't think like that, and that's the biggest reason he liked her.

So what he liked best about her might be his undoing. And he did like her. He might not be in a place in his life for a permanent relationship, but that didn't stop him from admiring her.

"You're taking this all wrong." No, you're *saying* it all wrong, a voice in his head chided. "I meant that when I look at you, I see a real person, not just an image you're trying to project."

She looked down at her muddy dress. "Yeah, definitely not the image I was going for tonight."

"I happen to like real people." He stalked over to her and lifted her chin with his thumb. "I happen to like you, Jade Fortune. Mud and all."

She swallowed. "Y-you do?"

"I do." His gaze landed on her parted lips. He needed another taste of that desirable, kissable mouth. The one sip of those exquisite lips at the coffee shop wasn't enough to satisfy his hunger. Would he ever get enough of this woman? "May I?"

She nodded and he leaned down and hovered with his mouth just above hers. He could feel her breath mingling with his. Heath eased forward until his lips touched hers, then cupped his palms around her face, angling her head so he could deepen the kiss. He drew the tip of his tongue along the seam of her lips and—

A howl pierced the air.

Jade pulled away and Heath let her go. The dog had ruined the moment, and he couldn't decide if Charlie's ill-timed interruption had spoiled his evening or had acted as a good reminder that this whole thing was fake. The engagement wasn't real, and he needed to remember that.

Charlie howled again and Heath knew why basset hounds had a reputation for being noisy. He'd researched the breed when he realized how important Charlie was to Jade.

He looked down at the dog. "Some wingman you turned out to be."

"Charlie, that was rude," Jade admonished.

"Maybe he doesn't like the idea of you kissing someone. Or is it *me*?" Talk about sounding needy. He hadn't anticipated wanting the approval of a dog. A woman's family maybe, but certainly not a floppy eared canine.

"He's never seen me kissing anyone," she admitted, then turned red as if realizing what her comment was revealing.

He couldn't prevent the grin spreading across his face. "That's good to know."

"Is it?" She suddenly smiled too.

"Yes, for sure." That bit of information, whether she'd wanted him to know it or not, made him happy. It probably shouldn't, because this wasn't real, but in this moment he didn't care.

"What about you?"

"I doubt Charlie has ever seen me kissing someone," he said, hoping to lighten the mood.

"Very funny. That's not what I meant."

"At my age, I've been in some relationships, but nothing terribly serious." Nothing that felt like this, and this—whatever this was growing between him and Jade—wasn't even a real relationship. Yet she was like a ray of sunshine cutting through the gray fog that had enveloped him since he'd started the quest to find out the truth about the circumstances of his birth. When he was with Jade, he wanted to know the truth of those circumstances for his own peace of mind. Jade might not care but he did.

Heath leaned toward her again, but Charlie shook himself, sending particles of dirt and mud flying.

"Yikes. I need to get him into a bath before he starts ruining everything. Ha! What am I saying? He's already ruined the evening."

As disappointed as he was, Heath wasn't going to let a dog chase him off. Even if that dog belonged to Jade. He was made of sterner stuff than that. "Nothing is ruined. Just modified."

"Modified?"

"Much of my best work was accomplished by running into a roadblock and having to alter my original plans." And that was the truth. One setback didn't mean the end.

"So you're not angry with the way this evening is going?"

"I got to kiss you…again. How could I be angry? And to set the record straight, I apologize for not asking before I kissed you the first time in the coffee shop. But the situation called for action. I hope you didn't mind."

"I had no objection." She shook her head slowly. "To be honest, I quite liked it."

He gave her a lopsided grin. "So did I."

Charlie chose that moment to lift his head and let out another long, loud howl. Maybe the basset hound was the smart one here, reminding them that this wasn't real.

"Charlie, no. Be quiet." Jade told him in a stern voice, but he continued to make noise. "He's doing this because he heard me say the word B-A-T-H."

"Charlie, quiet," he ordered.

The dog stopped and went over to Heath and sat.

"Good dog. Now, shake on it." Heath put out his hand and Charlie gave him his paw, but he'd forgotten the dog's paws were muddied. If he didn't know better, he'd swear that look Charlie gave him resembled a smirk. He'd bet the dog knew exactly what he was doing.

Heath stood and wiped his hand on his pants. They were already covered in dirt, so a little more wasn't going to matter.

"There," he said trying not to sound smug. "He's ready to get cleaned up."

"I don't believe it! What have you done with my dog?" Jade looked from Charlie to Heath and back. "If not for all that dirt, I'd think he was an impostor."

"You have to say it and mean it," Heath said, but he was as surprised as she that Charlie had obeyed him. And eternally grateful.

"Uh-huh, I'll try to remember that. Impostor or not, he needs to get clean." She turned her attention from the pooch to Heath. "Again, I'm sorry about the ruined evening."

"It's not ruined," he said and meant it. He was spending an evening with Jade; the rest was just window dressing. "We'll have something delivered and eat it here, if that's okay with you. You can give Charlie a bath while we wait."

True to form, Charlie howled at the word *bath*.

"Quiet," he said and held his breath.

The dog obeyed, but Heath decided he'd quit while he was ahead. He didn't want to push his luck. "I guess I proved my point. Now, about that delivery—"

"Delivery? Have you forgotten that this is Chatelaine?" Jade shook her head. "And if that isn't bad enough, the Fortune ranch is way off the beaten path. It'll be impossible to get someone out here."

"It's been my experience that nothing is impossible. I'll start calling around and see what I can come up with."

"You could, but why don't I save you the trouble? My mother sent over some homemade lasagna earlier today. I could heat that up, and I have the ingredients for a salad. If that is okay with you? The lasagna is big enough for two."

"More than okay. I can't remember the last time I had a home-cooked meal." But as far as he was concerned, any meal was a bonus to getting to spend an evening with Jade.

"Let me just get a towel so you can at least wipe off your pants. Sorry I don't have any spares to lend you."

"I've had worse on me. I test my gadgets in the real world of farms and ranches. A little mud from a dog is not that big a deal." And wasn't that the truth? Working ranches could be filthy, smelly places. But he liked to be hands-on with his projects. Hiring someone to do the dirty work for him didn't sit well with him. "Just point me in the direction of the bathroom, and I'll get washed up."

"Okay and I'll pop the lasagna in the oven, clean up Charlie and get changed. The lasagna should be heated through by then."

"Do you need any help?"

"No, thanks. It's bad enough Charlie got you dirty, you don't need him getting you wet too. Which is what would happen, believe me."

"Good point. I hope your dress isn't ruined." He'd only seen her wearing jeans, and he'd enjoyed that, but he had to admit it was also nice seeing her legs. She had sexy legs.

"Well, the dress says it's washable, so fingers crossed it all comes out."

"How about before I get cleaned up, I check out the yard and see what he got into. Not sure what I can do about a mud puddle, but I can make sure you don't have a leak of some sort. Or a break in your fence."

"Good idea. I hadn't thought of a break in the fencing. I'd hate for him to get out again if the backyard area isn't secure."

Heath nodded and let himself out the door she had used to let the dog in. He knew how fond she was of Charlie, and if he could prevent any harm coming to the dog, he'd do it. This so-called relationship might be fake, but he had to admit not all of his feelings for Jade were.

Jade leaned over and lathered up the dog, who complained with more than a few disgruntled snuffles and snorts. At least he didn't try to escape. Probably knew it was futile.

After her mother and sisters had left, she'd done the one thing she'd managed to resist despite her crush on Heath—she googled him. Besides lots of business articles about his successes with his company, she'd picked up a few more personal tidbits. Only one of them had her fretting.

Heath was thirty years old. That meant he was three years younger than her. It didn't matter. At least that's what she was telling herself. And it didn't. Not to her anyway. But what about Heath? He had to know. After all, he'd agreed to accompany her to her fifteenth-class reunion, so the math was simple. Could it be that he didn't mind?

After bathing the dog, she went into her bedroom and changed into dry clothes. Not exactly what she'd planned for the evening, but she found a white button-down blouse to pair with dry jeans. Maybe in some weird way, it was for the best, because she needed to remember the handsome entrepreneur was doing all this as a favor to her so she could save face with Nina and Alexis.

She found Heath in the kitchen, washing his hands at the sink. He turned and smiled at her as she walked in. At least he was still here. He hadn't stomped off when Charlie had gotten mud all over his pants.

"You had a bird bath that had gotten knocked over. That's what caused the puddle. I righted the bath and refilled it. You might want to supervise him until the puddle dries up."

"Thanks. I'll be sure to do that," she said as the timer went off on the stove. "The lasagna is almost done. It needs to sit on the counter for a few minutes so it will stay together when cut."

He helped her set the table and sliced cucumbers and tomatoes to add to the bagged salad she had on hand. She had to admit working alongside him in her kitchen was just as much fun as going to the country club. Maybe more so because she had Heath to herself for the evening.

Before they sat down to supper, she got a new chew bone out of one of the cabinets and handed it to Heath.

He accepted it with a raised eyebrow. "Thanks?"

"Maybe if you give it to him and tell him to go lay down with it, he'll obey."

Heath chuckled. "You're really putting me on the spot."

"You're the one with the special powers."

He showed Charlie the bone and brought it over to the dog bed in front of the fireplace. "This is for you to enjoy while we eat. Got that, buddy?"

Charlie took the bone and laid down to enjoy it. Heath glanced across to where she stood watching them.

"Impressive," she said. "It probably won't completely prevent him from begging for handouts at some point, but it might help some."

"You could have stopped at 'impressive,'" he said and made a noise with his tongue.

"Sorry," she said and set the casserole dish on the table.

"My reputation is in your paws, buddy," he told the dog and went to join Jade at the table.

The conversation came easily during supper. They decided to tell anyone who asked at the reunion that they'd seen one another when Heath came to Chatelaine on business. At least that was partly true. They'd been introduced last month when he first came to Chatelaine, but there was no need for them to go into an explanation about Heath looking for his half sisters and information about his biological father. That wasn't anyone else's business even if most people in Chatelaine knew he and the Perry triplets were half siblings.

"So, your sisters know the truth about this engagement?"

"Yeah, it would have been difficult to convince them I was truly engaged."

"Oh?"

"They know how important it is for me to find out the circumstances surrounding my birth before I could make that sort of commitment to anyone."

And especially to someone like her, Jade finished for him, channeling her father's voice. She needed to remember Heath was doing this as a favor for her. So she could save face after making that outrageous claim at the Daily Grind. If only she had kept her mouth shut, she wouldn't be in this mess now.

But was it really a mess? Or the most exciting thing to ever happen to her? The whole engagement might be a farce, but getting to spend time with Heath wasn't. She needed to learn to live in the moment, savor the present and let the future take care of itself.

The conversation had died down a bit after Heath made his pronouncement about needing to learn the truth about his birth before he could contemplate being in a serious relationship.

Not wanting the evening to end on a sour note, Jade decided to change the subject. "Tell me how you got Charlie to obey you so easily."

He exhaled as if he too was glad to change the subject. "It wasn't hard. I gave him a clear instruction and he obeyed."

"I know that but—"

"Haven't you done obedience training with him?" he interrupted with a frown.

"I have. Several times. He washed out each time." *A lot like me.* Thinking about her college days was too depressing, so she concentrated instead on the man she was spending the evening with. After all, growing up with Casper Windham and his brand of parenting, she'd had lots of practice pushing aside unpleasant thoughts.

"Maybe he obeyed because he knows I'm only temporary," he remarked.

She couldn't lie, his words hurt even if they were the truth. But she did her best to keep her emotions off her face and to keep her tone even. "Why would that matter?"

"I won't be around long enough to make him obey long term."

"I guess that makes sense." She needed to change the subject because the thought of not seeing Heath after the reunion was too depressing. "So, exactly what is it that you do for a living? I heard something about agricultural tech, but I'm not sure what that is."

"It means my company works with farmers and some ranchers to develop applications and tools."

"Doing what? Or is it a secret?" she asked.

He shook his head. "Not a secret in the broad sense. Some of our methods and equipment are proprietary, but not necessarily what the tools and apps do."

"Someone said something about using AI."

"Yeah, that's what we're working on now. I originally improved the weather apps used in farming equipment."

"Is that how you made all your money?" Jade slapped a hand over her mouth, but it was too late. The words were already out. "Oh, God, I'm so sorry. I didn't mean that. How gauche. Please ignore that. You don't have to answer."

Instead of being offended, he laughed. "It's okay. I already know I'm rich."

"That may be, but normally I have better manners."

Still smiling, he shook his head. "If it will make you feel any better, I can ask how it feels to find out you're a Fortune."

How was she supposed to answer that? She had all sorts of feelings, many of which were conflicting. "To be honest, I'm still getting used to it."

"But you changed your last name. It's my understanding that all of you changed from Windham to Fortune."

"Yes, we all did, but we did it more for our mother than any other reason. At least I did. Mom said it was entirely up to each of us, but I knew she really wanted it. I confess I didn't need a lot of convincing."

"Daddy issues?" he asked and flinched. "Now it's

my turn to be gauche. I apologize. It's really none of my business."

Just goes to show that this isn't a real relationship, Jade thought. If they really were engaged, he wouldn't be saying that. They'd feel free to share things like that with one another.

She sighed. It was true that she still had a lot of unresolved issues involving Casper Windham. At first, she'd balked at the idea of changing her last name but came to the consensus her siblings did that her mother was here, and their dad wasn't. She didn't want to damage her relationship with her only living parent. Not that her mother would have pushed. "It's complicated, but you're not far off."

"Would it help to talk about it?"

"I don't know. It's probably pretty boring, and I don't like to play the poor little rich girl card." Even during those years after high school when she'd been drifting, she knew she was lucky. She had family and resources to fall back on. That's why now, when she'd finally landed on her feet, she did all she could to help the kids who attended her day camps.

"That's right. You were rich even before you became a Fortune," Heath was saying. "Your dad was Windham Plastics."

She couldn't have put it better herself. Her dad lived and breathed his company, even to the point of ignoring his family. But the business was why she had the resources to do what she, her mother and her siblings were now doing, so she had no right to complain. But that didn't prevent some feelings of resentment when she thought about her father and his attitude toward her. "It meant everything to him."

"Ah, I'm getting a vibe here. Does some of that have to do with the tension I sense when Casper is mentioned?"

"You could say that," she acknowledged.

His lips twisted into a grimace. "Not that I'm defending him, but businesses take a lot of time and care... successful ones even more. And from what I understand, Windham Plastics was extremely successful."

"It was, and I know I shouldn't complain since it gave my brothers and sisters and me a comfortable upbringing. We were able to move to Chatelaine and make the Fortune family ranch into something we can all be proud of."

"From what I hear, you have every right to be proud of the petting zoo."

She laughed, unsure if he was serious. "Right."

"I'm serious. Between that and the camps and workshops you're doing, you have a chance to change the lives of a lot of children in Chatelaine."

"Thank you, but I hardly think I'm changing lives." She shook her head. Sure, she enjoyed what she was doing, and she was doing her best to adhere to ethical guidelines when it came to the animals in her care, but she doubted she was transforming anyone's life but her own. She wasn't struggling to find her place anymore and that felt good. Which was why she felt baffled by her behavior in front of Alexis and Nina. Seeing them and listening to them had thrown her back into the dark days of high school. And she'd managed to drag Heath into her drama.

"Don't be too sure. Programs like yours changed my life, and look where I am today."

She pulled back in surprise. "You can't be serious."

"But I am. As the child of a single mother, there wasn't a lot of extra money, but I was able to enjoy attending free lectures similar to the ones you sponsor. That sparked my interest in technology being used for farming and ranching."

"So, maybe I'm creating your competition with my little camps?" she teased.

He laughed, sending tingles down her spine. She couldn't remember any man causing her spine to tingle. She liked it. A lot. Maybe that explained her behavior at the Daily Grind.

"I'll forgive you. There's room for everyone," Heath told her.

"That's pretty magnanimous of you."

Grinning, he shrugged. "It'll be a few years yet before I'll be looking over my shoulder. The ones you teach are pretty young still."

"Yes, but you're pretty young to be such a success as well." *And to be so rich*, she thought and frowned. That truly didn't matter to her.

"Are there any kids that stand out that I should be worried about?"

"Well—" she dragged out the word "—there is one that's quite smart. His name is Billy Connor. He lost his dad about a year ago, and his mom has been bringing him around a lot."

"I'd be happy to meet with him, if you want."

"I'll bet he'll be thrilled," she said without thinking.

She'd been concerned about Billy. She knew him as a quiet and respectful boy, but lately he'd been disruptive during her presentations.

He frowned. "Forgive me. Did I sound pompous?"

"What? No. Sorry. My mind was elsewhere for a minute. Billy hasn't been himself lately, and I'm not sure why. I didn't mean to come across as sarcastic." The last thing she wanted to do was take out her frustrations on Heath.

He touched her arm. "I have a feeling we're both a little on edge."

"It's all my fault for opening my big mouth and claiming we're engaged," she said thickly.

He lightly squeezed her arm. "Considering I went along with you, I'd say we're in this together."

"I'm not such a martyr as to accept the full blame if you're willing to accept half." She laughed, feeling much lighter. "So, yes, I suppose we are in this together."

"Maybe we need to establish some ground rules," he said abruptly, dropping his hand.

She missed the warmth of his touch. "Ground rules?"

Of course he wanted ground rules. Her head may have been in the clouds regarding this fake engagement, but his certainly wasn't. And why should it be? *He* wasn't spinning dreams around her rash statement. *She* was the one doing that.

Jade pushed those unproductive thoughts aside and inhaled, waiting for what Heath was going to say.

Don't buy trouble, she told herself.

He drew his hands through his hair and, after a long

palpable moment, finally spoke. "I like you and want to be honest with you, Jade."

"I like you too, and I'm all for honesty." She might want the truth, but that didn't prevent his words from causing her to feel a bit anxious about what he might say next. Sounded like trouble was coming of its own accord.

"I want to explain what I meant when I said I didn't want to get involved."

"If you don't want to get involved, that's your right. You don't have to explain—"

"But I want to because you're special, Jade."

Oh my. His words did funny things to her insides. She didn't think anyone had ever called her special before.

Before she could respond, he continued. "You know that the Perry triplets are my sisters—well, half sisters."

She managed a shaky smile. Just because he'd called her special didn't negate the fact that he was explaining why he didn't want to get too deeply involved with her. At least he offered an explanation. A lot more than most guys would. Maybe this wouldn't be so bad after all. It wasn't like he was telling her anything she didn't already know. "I think the entire town knows."

"Yes, well, like I said, I'm trying to find out the true reason I never knew about them, nor they about me. I realize their circumstances probably made it impossible since they were so young when their parents died. But my mother also never told me the truth."

"How did you find out that you even had sisters?" Having grown up with her five siblings, she could not imagine what it would be like to only discover them now as an adult. Her heart went out to him and his sisters.

"After my mother passed, I realized I would never get any answers from her, so I took a DNA test. I was matched with one of my sisters. Fortunately, I was able to contact her and found out I had not just one but three sisters." He shook his head, his expression conveying he was focused on something only he could see.

This time it was she who reached out to touch him. "I can't imagine how that must feel, but I'm glad you've finally found one another."

He seemed to come back to himself and turned his attention back to her. "Yeah, it answers some questions but raises a bunch more."

Those questions probably had to do with his biological father. Did he hope to find answers here? "So, finding your sisters is how you ended up in Chatelaine?"

He sighed. "Yeah. We've been trying to find out what happened, but it hasn't been easy."

"Have you been able to learn anything about the circumstances surrounding your birth?" For all the problems she'd experienced in the fraught relationship with her father, at least she'd had one. She and he hadn't had time to settle any differences between them before he died, but that didn't weigh as heavily on her now as it once had. She still minded, but not nearly as much.

"We've managed to learn very little. Doris Edwards— I'm not sure if you know her—knew my mother before I was born. She's a greeter a couple days a week at Great-Store. Except the woman is now suffering from bouts of dementia and isn't always lucid. For example, she told my sisters that we were quadruplets, but that's impossible because I was born two months before them and in a different town. Those are undisputed facts. My sister Haley confronted her, and she claimed that my parents were taking me to the hospital the night they were killed in that accident. But that's impossible unless my mother lied to me. As an infant, I would not have been in Chatelaine. I would have been with her in Cactus Grove. It makes no sense."

"I'm sure the DNA would show you're not full brother and sister." She could tell that he was bothered by all this conflicting information, and she couldn't blame him.

"Yes, so I knew going in that they were going to be half siblings, but I still want to know what happened. This Doris woman seemed to be the only one who knew there were four of us babies fathered by the same man."

"But she hasn't been able to explain how?" Jade wished she could help him. He had stood up for her when she made her engagement claim, and she wanted to return the favor. But how?

"Not yet. But I'm not giving up. She has her lucid moments, and she's indicated that knows something even if she can't remember exactly what she knows."

"Quite a conundrum."

He laughed. "Yeah, that's one way of putting it."

"So, exactly how does this affect our situation?" She called it a "situation" because she wasn't sure how else to refer to it.

"I'm good with keeping up the pretense of us being engaged until after your reunion."

But don't make the mistake of thinking it's real, she finished for him.

She needed to repeat that as a mantra because her simple crush on Heath Blackwood was starting to feel like something more. Something real. Something dangerous to her heart.

Chapter Five

Heath winced. What was he doing pouring his heart out to Jade? Like she'd be interested in all his birth mystery drama. He was pretty sure Jade's two classmates would have fled the scene by now, bored to tears. Or they would have offered empty platitudes before steering the conversation to something else.

But not Jade. She expressed genuine interest and sympathy, he argued with himself.

While he was engaged in his internal debate, she got up and started to pick up their dirty dishes.

Remembering his manners, he stood and picked up his plate. "Here, let me help."

"That's not necessary."

"I insist. You fed me. I'll help clean up." He wasn't so far removed from his humble beginnings that kitchen work was beneath him. His merit scholarships didn't always cover his living expenses or books, and he'd bussed tables to earn money during college.

"But it was my dog that ruined the date."

"Will you stop saying he ruined it. Poor guy's going to get a complex. He didn't ruin our evening. Unless..." Had she wanted to go to the LC Club? Maybe he was wrong about Jade not caring about appearances. He hoped he was wrong.

She frowned. "Unless what?"

"Maybe you would have preferred going to the country club? Would you have preferred being seen tonight?"

"Being *seen*? I don't understand what you mean by that." Her tone held a note of suspicion.

"Some women prefer getting dressed up and going out so they can be seen by others." He might be insulting her with his assumptions, but he needed to know before he got too involved.

Wait. What was he thinking? He had no plans to get involved beyond a few dates and the reunion. He was going to say something to that effect, but she was already answering him.

"Believe me, that's not me. I got dressed up because I didn't want to embarrass you, but the part about being seen doesn't interest me in the least."

"Let's get one thing straight. Jade Fortune, you would never embarrass me. I'm proud to be seen with you, whether you're wearing jeans or a dress." And that was the truth. He found her refreshing and he was relieved by her attitude.

She gave him a look he wasn't sure how to interpret and nodded once. "Thanks. How about I make some coffee, and we can take it to the back patio? The moon is pretty full tonight, so we might even see it reflected off the lake."

"Sounds great. Your place really is well situated here," he said as he stacked the last plate into the dishwasher and closed it. "Do you want to run the dishwasher?"

"Yeah." She rummaged in the cabinet under the sink and pulled out a detergent packet, put it into the holder in the door and started it. Going to the faucet, she ran water into an electric teakettle.

He grimaced at the thought of instant coffee, but to his relief, she pulled a French press off the shelf under the kitchen island. While the water heated, she measured ground coffee into the pot.

Heath watched her quick, economical movements. Once again, he found himself contemplating her hands. They were unadorned but they fascinated him. He frowned when he recalled that one woman's comment about Jade not having a ring despite the engagement. Well, he'd have to do something about that before the high school reunion. He took a closer look at her fingers. That's when he noticed a nasty cut on her index finger. "How did you do that?"

"Do what?" Jade asked as she measured ground coffee into the French press.

He took her hand in both of his. "That looks like a serious cut."

"Not bad enough for stitches, but I did some serious bleeding."

"I hope you're up to date on your tetanus shot."

She rolled her eyes. "Of course. I live on a ranch and work at a petting zoo."

Yeah, he got it. He was making a fool of himself, but he couldn't help worrying about her. Instead of responding, he brought her hand to his lips and kissed it before letting go.

They stood facing one another, neither one speaking.

Finally, Heath cleared his throat and stepped back. He needed to stop this. Getting involved too deeply with anyone at this time wasn't a good idea. Once again, he reminded himself that finding out the truth about his father and the mystery surrounding his birth was his first priority.

But what if he didn't like what he found? He pushed the disturbing thought aside. First things first.

"Let me finish getting the coffee ready," she said and turned away, busying herself with pouring the hot water over coffee grounds and stirred. She replaced the plunger into the pot and set it aside to steep.

"I see you have some torches around the patio. Would you like me to light them?"

"That would be great. Most have citronella to help ward off bugs." She opened a drawer and pulled out a barbecue stick lighter.

They sat in comfortable wooden rockers facing the lake with a small table between their chairs. The flickering torches gave the setting a warm ambience. Even better than an evening dining and dancing at the country club. The one downside was that without dancing, he didn't have an excuse to hold her in his arms. There were always other times, he consoled himself.

"Is there something I should know about you before the reunion?" Jade asked. "I know about your job and family, but I'm talking about something that might not be common knowledge. Like Twizzlers or Red Vines?"

"Neither. What about you?"

She shot him a look. "What? How is something like that even possible?"

"Because I'm more of a Jelly Belly guy," he said and waited for her reaction.

"Ooh, I like those too. All those flavors. I guess I'll have to give you a pass on the licorice."

"Damn right, you will." The conversation might be silly, but he was enjoying sitting with Jade and wanted to know more about her. "Aside from this thing about red licorice, is there anything else I should know about you?"

She sighed. "If you must know, my phone is full of pictures of Charlie."

"So?" He stifled the laugh that bubbled up. The only light on the patio came from the torches, but from what he could see, she was blushing. He couldn't remember the last time he'd been with a woman who blushed. He quite liked it.

Her eyes widened. "You don't think that's strange?"

"Should I?"

"I'm sure Nina and Alexis would think so."

"Why should you care what they think?"

Yeah, why *should* she, Jade wondered. Heath had a point. She shrugged. "I guess that day in the coffee shop, I was thrown back into high school."

He shook his head. "Those of us who weren't popular in high school have moved on. Some people reached their peak back then. That's the real shame. Their glory days are behind them. On the other hand, ours are ahead of us."

"I'm not sure I have glory days ahead of me, but thanks for thinking so."

He made a sound with his tongue. "Don't discount

what you're doing, Jade. How do you think I got my start?"

"At a petting zoo?"

He chuckled, sending her pulse racing.

He turned toward her. "All those workshops you do. Like I said before, I attended some like that when I was young, and it encouraged me to pursue my dreams of using technology to help farmers and ranchers."

Her eyes widened. "You seriously did attend ones like I give?"

"I haven't been to any of yours, so I don't know if they're exactly the same, but I'm sure you could be inspiring the next generation of innovative farmers and ranchers."

"The next Heath Blackwoods, you mean?"

He laughed and touched the end of her nose.

"Are you still interested in speaking at one of my workshops?"

"Of course. I'd love to," he replied. "Just let me know when and I'll be there."

"Thank you so much. This will mean a lot to the kids."

He flashed her a grin. "I'm not sure they'll even know who I am, but I'm happy to help."

That grin made her heart do some sort of stumble thing but she managed one of her own. Albeit a shaky one.

"Right," he said with a glance at her mouth before continuing, "I'd better get going."

With that he gave her a distracted nod, turned, and left, leaving her wondering if that last part was meant for her or himself.

After Heath left for the evening, Jade knew she was going to have to remember that this was a fake engagement. She needed to keep that in mind at all times or risk getting her heart broken. Heath was doing her a favor by going along with the fake engagement. She might be falling for him, but he was definitely not falling for her, and she'd do well to remember that.

Charlie came over, stood next to her and whined, deep in his throat.

"Don't you start falling for him too," she cautioned him.

The next morning, while Jade went about her chores at the Fortune Family Petting Zoo, the previous night's date kept crowding out her other thoughts. She had to acknowledge that her little crush on Heath Blackwood was no longer little. And that could create a problem. A *big* one.

It wasn't easy, but she pushed thoughts of Heath out of her head so she could concentrate on her project. She had turned an old, disused aluminum rowboat into a small pond with a fountain.

Jade turned on the water pump to be sure it worked. Thankfully it did, and the water in the aluminum rowboat and water sprayed up through the small fountain she'd placed in the middle. The boat was battered, but she'd repaired the rust spot enough for the craft to hold water. While the rowboat might not be lake worthy, it made a wonderful swimming pool for the ducks.

"What a clever idea."

Jade turned to see Hope standing there watching the proceedings with avid interest.

"Thanks," she said and wiped her hands on her jeans. "I saw an example of this online and thought I'd try it for the baby ducks."

"I love it. Can't wait for Evie to see it with ducks in it."

Jade glanced around but Hope seemed to be alone. "Speaking of Evie, where is she?"

"Ridge has her. She's fascinated by the baby chicks in the incubator." She smiled. "Your brother is very good with her."

"I know," Jade said.

It never ceased to amaze her how comfortable Ridge was with the baby. He'd taken to fatherhood like…well, like a duck to water. Except he wasn't that baby's father. And that was what bothered her, because he could be heading for a world of hurt if he didn't put the brakes on.

Pot? Kettle?

Yeah, she didn't have room to criticize. Look at the dangerous game she was playing with Heath. He wasn't really her fiancé, and no amount of wishing was going to make that true. He'd rescued her from humiliation in front of those snotty girls and was doing her a favor by taking her to the reunion. But she needed to remember that when the clock struck midnight, her carriage would turn back into a pumpkin.

"So, I thought I'd take a moment to explain…"

Hope's words brought Jade back to the here and now. "Explain what?"

"What happened at the coffee shop?"

Jade shook her head. "That's not necessary."

"No. I don't want you to think I'm some sort of flake. Freaking out the way I did." Hope heaved a sigh.

"I would never think that."

"All I remember is that when that woman started chasing after her child, I panicked. I had a memory flash of a middle-aged couple smiling at Evie but suddenly turning mean and saying I had to hand my baby over." Hope shuddered.

Jade put her arm around the other woman, hoping to comfort her. She didn't know what else to do. Saying everything was going to be okay sounded disingenuous because Jade had no idea what had happened in Hope's past. Without knowing the woman's situation, how could she be sure things would work out? Jade was convinced that Hope was Evie's mother, but that fact alone didn't mean she had rightful custody of the baby. Any number of things could have happened.

"I know it was just a memory surfacing, but it scared me," Hope was saying and pulled Jade back to the conversation.

"I can understand how that could happen. Please, don't think anything of it." Especially after what she herself had done in that coffee shop. People could react in extreme ways in certain situations.

"There you are," Ridge strolled over and stood beside Hope. He had Evie securely on his hip, his arm around her. "See? Mommy is right here. I told you she couldn't have gotten far," he crooned to the baby.

Evie reached out her chubby arms to Hope, who took her from Ridge and hugged her close.

Ridge gave Jade a playful swat on the shoulder. "Hey, Sis."

"How's it going?" Jade asked, hoping she'd managed to keep the doom and gloom she felt over his situation from her voice.

"Great. Did you put this together?" he asked, pointing to the makeshift duck pond.

Jade puffed out her chest. "I did."

"So that's why you wanted that old boat." He squatted on his heels to examine her creation.

"I told you I had a use for it," she said, waiting to see if he found anything wrong.

"You did, and I confess I lacked the imagination to picture this."

"I guess I was a bit vague in my explanation. I wanted to be sure I could pull it off." She was so used to being a failure in front of her family that it was old habit to keep things from them.

Ridge stood. "Well, you certainly pulled it off. Great job."

Jade smiled. She really had found her calling with this petting zoo.

Ridge chucked her on the shoulder. "But was there ever any doubt?"

"I imagine there was a lot. I haven't exactly been the most successful member of this family."

Ridge gave his sister a quick one-armed hug. "*Pfft.* So what if you took a little longer to find your way? You're doing a bang-up job with the zoo and the day camps for kids."

"Thanks." It felt good having her family see her as successful.

"Uh-oh, I think this little girl needs a diaper change," Hope said and wrinkled her nose. "How such a sweet thing can make such a big stink is beyond me."

"You can take her over to the family area. We have facilities there." Jade pointed to a small outbuilding painted barn red.

Ridge watched Hope walk off, then turned to Jade. "Did she say anything more to you about what happened at the Daily Grind? I know she felt bad leaving like that. She insisted on coming to explain."

"She apologized again, but I assured her it was okay. I guess something someone said sparked a partial memory. Has she regained any more substantial recollections?"

He nodded. "After we got home and we were unpacking the diaper bag, she had another flash."

Jade noticed how he'd casually used the word *home*. She knew they weren't living together, because Hope and the baby were in a small cabin close to Ridge's. But the way he'd said it indicated to Jade that he was getting deeper and deeper with Hope. "Can you tell me about it?" she asked.

"It wasn't very detailed, but she said she recalled throwing things in Evie's baby bag and rushing to a car. She remembers constantly checking the rearview mirror as she drove away."

Jade put her hand on her brother's arm. His muscles were bunched stiff. "Oh no, Ridge. This sounds pretty serious."

He shook his head and looked at Jade, a bleak expression in his eyes. "Sounds like she was running from someone. But who? An abusive husband?"

"Give her time and space. I'm sure her memories will come back." Jade wished she could believe her own words. But what else could she do? Ridge was an adult. All she could do was pray things would work out for him. If not, she and the rest of the family would be there for him.

"Thanks. I'm sure they will too."

They were silent for a moment.

"I'm just afraid what those memories will reveal," he whispered, "but I'm all in no matter what happens."

Jade squeezed her brother's hand. Even when she was drifting along trying to find her place in the world, her siblings had been there for her. No matter what Casper said or did, Jade knew she could count on her brothers and sisters. "You know we'll be here for you and Hope and baby Evie. No matter what."

"It looks like this might work out," Jade said as she watched Dahlia's lamb exploring the new enclosure Jade had built when her sister had approached her about the lamb.

"It's not a permanent solution, but I'm glad to have someplace safe for it," Dahlia said.

Her younger sister had been taking care of a lamb that had been rejected by its mother. Jade had two other lambs, and Dahlia thought being with others might help the baby. They stood by the fence and watched the lambs getting to know one another.

"Has Ridge said anything more about what's been going on with Hope?" Dahlia asked curiously.

"He and Hope were here this morning with the baby." Jade debated how much to say but, in the end, opted for the truth. Ridge was Dahlia's baby brother too.

"I just pray he knows what he's getting into with all this," Dahlia muttered after Jade had told her what she knew.

"Me too."

"Speaking of relationships, I saw Heath driving through town this morning," Dahlia said.

"Huh." Jade's stomach tightened. Had Heath said something to her sister? "Did you talk to him?"

"No. I didn't get a chance to do more than wave. I was coming out of the feed store when he went by."

Jade nodded, secretly relieved that they didn't have a chance to chat.

"But Phyllis did. Talk, that is."

Jade groaned.

"Yeah, she asked all about you. Kept asking me about the engagement and how sudden it was. Seems you were in the feed store gabbing with her and didn't mention anything about an engagement even when she mentioned Heath's name to you."

"What did you say?" Jade hated putting her family on the spot, but there wasn't much she could do about her impulsive lie at the moment.

"I reminded her what a private person you were," Dahlia said and grinned.

"And did she believe you?"

Her sister noisily blew air between her lips. "Hardly.

So I started talking about Rawlston, and she took the bait, asking all sorts of intrusive questions. You owe me, big-time."

Jade winced. It wasn't that long ago when Dahlia and Rawlston were the hot topic when they came back from Vegas married, of all things. Everything worked out in the end, and they were deliriously happy now. But some people still liked to speculate on what actually happened in Vegas.

"Doesn't Phyllis know that what happens in Vegas stays in Vegas?"

"Evidently not."

Jade heaved a sigh. "Sorry about that. Like you said, I owe you."

Dahlia leaned against the fence and turned her head to look at Jade. "Then tell me what's bothering you?"

"What makes you think something is bothering me?"

"Because you had a weird look on your face when I mentioned Heath. Are you two still planning to go through with the trip to the reunion?"

"Yes. Mom has agreed to watch Charlie while I'm gone. It's only for the day, but you know I don't like leaving him on his own without some backup plan." And considering what had happened when she'd let him into the yard unsupervised the other night, she had all the more reason to be concerned.

Dahlia grinned. "Yes, we all know he's your baby. At least for the time being."

"What's that supposed to mean?"

"Nothing, except I'm sure some day you'll get married and have human babies too."

Jade wished she could be as confident about her future as Dahlia seemed to be. She was happy with her life as it was, but that didn't mean she didn't want a family of her own someday.

"C'mon, Sis, spill it. I can tell something's on your mind."

At the risk of having her sister laugh, Jade told the truth. "I realized I'm three years older than Heath."

Dahlia gasped. "Oh my God! How did I not know about this shocking bit of information?"

Jade opened her mouth to speak, but Dahlia beat her to it. "I don't understand why you felt you weren't able to confide in us. I mean, this is just shocking. My sister, a cradle robber."

"Very funny. Are you done?" Okay, maybe she was making more of this than was necessary. Three years wasn't much at all. And she probably wouldn't even have thought much of it if she hadn't also wondered why Heath was interested in her. But she wasn't gorgeous like her sisters or sophisticated like Alexis and Nina. No matter what she did, she couldn't rid herself of the awkward girl she used to be. That girl was buried deep inside Jade.

"Am I done? Hmm, let me think." Dahlia tilted her head to the side and tapped a finger on her cheek.

"Dahlia," Jade said, a note of warning in her voice.

"Okay, I guess that's all I've got. If I come up with something else, you'll be the first to know."

"I can hardly wait." She snorted. "Maybe you should take that show on the road."

"C'mon, Jade. Lighten up." Dahlia playfully bumped

shoulders with her. "And seriously, three years is not a big deal."

"What if he thinks it is?" That's what had been bothering her. What did *Heath* think about it? Why hadn't he mentioned it?

"He must know it if he's agreed to take you to your fifteenth high school reunion. I'm sure he's done the math. Have you asked him?"

"No."

"Why? Afraid of the answer?" Dahlia asked.

Jade rolled her eyes but didn't respond, because her sister had gotten it right.

"He must've known when he told those brats that he was going to the reunion with you. Face it, Jade, the man is a genius. I'm sure he can do math in his head. Has he said anything about it?"

"No." But then neither had she.

Dahlia shook her head at Jade. "Then why are you turning it into an issue? If it's because someone else said something, then stop this nonsense right now."

"Nonsense?"

"Yeah. Until or unless you hear directly from Heath that the age gap matters to him, it's a nonissue."

Dahlia made sense and Jade wanted to believe her. And she did…mostly. Still, there was that small part of her, the part where Casper's caustic remarks took up residence, that found it hard to believe Heath didn't care.

Chapter Six

Heath looked up from the laptop on his table on the porch at the Daily Grind. He was beginning to think of this table as his spot since he'd taken to spending time drinking coffee and doing research here. Plus, it reminded him of his first official meeting with Jade. Both a blessing and a curse. He loved spending time with her, but it was getting harder and harder to keep in mind that theirs was a fake relationship.

Today, like the other day, he'd taken advantage of the spot to conduct some research and some business, such as answering business emails. He couldn't let his personal searches regarding his past overshadow his business concerns. After all, he'd worked too hard to get where he was to let this issue cause him to lose his edge over the competition.

He glanced across the porch to see his sister Lily. She was climbing the steps to the porch. Spotting him, she waved.

"I thought I might catch you here," she said as she approached the table.

"I didn't realize you were looking for me." He stood and gave her a quick hug.

"I was at the feed store and spotted your SUV, so I decided to take a detour and come here before heading back home."

"Well, I'm glad you did."

"Have you made any progress?" she asked, hitching her chin toward his laptop.

He knew she meant in his research regarding their biological father. "No. I think I've just about exhausted anything I can find online. I'm thinking about taking another shot at Doris Edwards. Maybe I can catch her in a lucid moment."

"We could try that, or maybe we should talk to her daughter," Lily said. "Phyllis at the feed store said her daughter has been caring for her mother for the past year. Veronica takes her mother to and from work."

"I still find it surprising that the woman still holds down a job." He knew Doris was still employed by the GreatStore.

"She likes it and I imagine greeting people as they come in to shop is good for her. Besides, it's only a few hours a day and a couple days a week. I'm glad the management of the store allows it."

Heath nodded. "Chatelaine seems like the kind of place that takes care of its own."

As little as six months ago, he would not have seen himself living in such a small town without the conveniences he was accustomed to, like twenty-four-hour food delivery. Although the evening with Jade had been enjoyable, thanks to her. He even smiled a little as he remembered one of those women who'd been snotty to Jade had likened the place to a vast wasteland because it lacked a Nordstrom. But since getting involved with Jade, he had grown to like the place, and settling here permanently no longer seemed like such an outlandish idea. These days, with the internet and various technologies to connect people, working from a remote location, even one as remote and small as Chatelaine, was very doable.

"I can contact Veronica, if you'd like. I was on a parade committee with her last year and have her number."

"Do you think she can give answers that Doris won't or can't?" Was finding out about his past going to be that simple? He cautioned himself not to get his hopes up. They'd been dashed enough times already.

His sister shrugged. "I don't know, but it's worth a shot."

Lily pulled out her phone and thumbed through her contacts. "I'll arrange a meeting for you with her."

She smiled at him while she waited for her call to go through. He thought about how lucky he'd been with his sisters. They'd readily accepted him and had set about forging bonds despite only learning about a brother after they'd found one another. Lily, Tabitha and Haley had been separated as babies after the tragic death of their parents and had also come together as adults. But as full-blooded sisters and triplets to boot, their bond was much stronger. His link to them was more tenuous, especially since they didn't know why he'd never been told about them or his father. Perhaps if the cancer hadn't taken his mother so quickly after being diagnosed, Anne might have given him an explanation. But that didn't happen, and he had to accept it.

Lily ended her call and looked at him. "Veronica says she can meet with you this afternoon at the real estate office where she works."

"Will you—" He stopped and cleared his throat. "Would you like to come with me? This involves all of us."

There. Phrasing it that way didn't sound quite so needy. Not that he wouldn't go alone. He'd been doing things by himself most of his life. His mother had worked two jobs to put a roof over their heads and food on the table. He'd helped out as soon as he was able, and of course once his start-up company was making a profit, he'd done his best to make his mom's life comfortable, but the cancer had taken her so quickly. He hadn't had a chance to do all the things for her that he'd wanted.

"Sure." Lily dropped her phone back into her purse. "I'd love to come. I know Haley and Tabitha are both busy today, but I'll let them know if we find out anything worthwhile."

"We have some time to kill, so why don't you sit and have something while I finish my coffee."

"Sounds good. Let me go to the window and order something."

Heath jumped up, "Let me get it. A thank-you for coming with me today."

"No thanks necessary. We're family."

Warmth bloomed in his chest at her simple statement. Lily told him what she wanted, and he went to place her order. As he waited next to the walk-up window, his gaze went to his sister sitting at the table. He'd told Jade that he wasn't ready for a committed relationship while the story of his birth was still a mystery, but he wondered now if that was completely true. He treasured his burgeoning relationship with the triplets. So what made his feelings regarding Jade so complicated?

Maybe they'd learn something important today from Doris's daughter, and he could figure out his feelings for his fake fiancée.

He picked up Lily's mocha latte and brought it to their table. As they sipped their drinks, they talked about ranching and some ideas Heath had for devices to make life easier for ranchers. Heath had worked closely with Lily's husband, Asa Fortune. Asa's ranch was a dude ranch, but he and Heath had thrown some serious ideas around. Today's meeting loomed, but neither wanted to dwell on what-ifs.

The real estate office where Veronica worked was located along the main street in Chatelaine. Veronica was alone in the office when they arrived. After greeting and seating them around a small table in what looked like a conference area, she offered them coffee.

Lily chuckled. "We just came from the Daily Grind, but thanks anyway."

"I can't compete with the fancy stuff they sell anyway. We only recently upgraded to one of those coffee makers that uses those coffee pods," Veronica said with a smile.

"Yeah, we're lucky to have such a great coffee shop in Chatelaine," Lily murmured.

Lily's comment threw Heath back to the day Jade claimed they were engaged. She had defended the town's somewhat unusual coffee shop.

Yes, he was on this journey of discovery for himself and his siblings, but Jade and a possible future with her was always there in the back of his mind.

"I'm not sure why my mother has told you the things she has, but I need to clear up some of what she's been saying," Veronica said, not wasting time on small talk.

"You mean the things she's been saying about me as a baby being with my father? That bit of information had shaken me the most," he said. If it were true, why hadn't his mother ever mentioned it?

Veronica nodded; her features masked in sadness. "About you and that night. The night your father was killed, one of my mother's neighbors came to ask if I could come over and babysit her daughter. Megan Shaw lived next door and I occasionally babysat her six-year-old daughter Tiffany. Megan's husband had been hurt at work, and she needed to go to him at the hospital. The woman was pretty upset and worried. So was Mom. Anyway, as it turns out, that was the night James Perry and his wife were also killed. I didn't know it at the time, but Mom knew about him because of her friend Anne. Your mother. I think she's confused the two things in her mind."

"Well, that makes sense," Lily said and glanced at Heath as if for confirmation.

He nodded, trying to digest this information. At least he now knew his mother hadn't kept this tidbit of information a secret from him. It seemed more logical that if she left Chatelaine, she hadn't had any more contact with James Perry. Of course that didn't mean she never told him that he had a son. That was still a possibility, depending on the nature of their relationship. Or their *lack* of one. Perhaps the simplest explanation was a one-night stand, but that didn't explain how close in age he was to his half sisters.

"I'm sorry if she's upset you or made things more difficult," Veronica said.

Heath shook his head. "It's not her fault. I'm just sorry she's so confused. I know how hard it is when it's your mom that's being ravaged by a cruel disease."

Veronica's expression told him how much she appreciated his words. "If I could help you, I would, but I didn't pay a lot of attention to that sort of gossip at that age. I was more into boys and clothes. I babysat to earn money to buy clothes. But what am I doing telling you all this stuff? Not like you're interested. I just wanted you to know I'd help if I could."

"You've already helped by debunking the story about me being with my father that night."

Veronica nodded. "I can talk to my mom about Anne and let you know if she tells me anything new. She has good days and bad. If I can catch her on a good day, I might be able to find out something. She has talked a few times about a memory box, but I have no idea what she means. I'm sorry."

"Thanks, we really appreciate your time," Heath murmured.

A telephone rang in the outer office.

"Sorry, but I need to get that," Veronica said and rose from her seat.

"We won't keep you any longer." Heath and Lily both stood, and he reached out his hand toward Veronica.

"Thanks again. We know this isn't easy on anyone and we appreciate your willingness to help."

After they got back into his SUV, Heath sat for a moment and looked at the modest brick ranch home typical of the sixties and seventies that had been turned into a real estate office. But he wasn't really seeing the house. This had been another dead end. Did Doris even know his mother? It's not as if Anne ever talked about her or even her time in Chatelaine. It wasn't until his DNA was matched with the triplets that he was aware of the dusty little town.

Would he ever find out the truth so he could put it behind him? He groaned.

A hand touched his arm. He was startled. He'd almost forgotten that Lily was with him. Poor girl. He always seemed to be dragging her into his drama.

"It's a setback but not a dead end," she told him.

He ground his back teeth. He didn't want sympathy, but instead of reacting, he inhaled deeply. Lily was his sister, one of the only relatives he had, and he didn't want to do anything to alienate her. And if he succeeded in damaging his relationship with her, his relationship with his other sisters would suffer too. That was the last thing he wanted. He found he quite liked being a big brother. Not something he ever thought he'd be.

"Thanks for coming with me today," he mumbled and gave her a quick hug.

She patted his chest. "No thanks necessary. We're family now."

He turned his head and met her gaze. His chest tightened with emotions he couldn't name. Maybe they didn't grow up together and were bound together by a man neither of them had known, but none of that mattered now that they'd found one another. Their bond was unbreakable. "We are, aren't we?"

"Growing up, I always dreamed of having a family." She laughed. "And now I seem to have them coming out of my ears."

"I'm going to assume that's a good thing."

"Very. I'm definitely not complaining." She nodded with a smile. "What about you? Are you happy to have extended family?"

"I am." He might still be getting used to having sisters in his life, but he was grateful for them.

After dropping Lily off, Heath ran an errand, then headed for the Fortune Family Ranch. He didn't think he'd gotten his hopes up, but the disappointment he was feeling belied his thoughts. Maybe seeing Jade and talking with her would help him put things in perspective. Knowing he'd be in her presence soon lifted his spirits. He patted the box in his pocket and glanced at the back seat to what he'd put there a few moments ago.

A faint voice in his head issued a warning that all he and Jade had was a fake relationship. Something based on a lie. So why did it feel so real when he kissed her?

He chose to ignore the voice and the warning. For now.

"Charlie, will you please let me put this on you," Jade pleaded, but the dog once again managed to wriggle out of the Sherlock Hound costume before she could get it fastened.

She'd purchased the getup off a website and now wondered what drugs they'd given the dog who'd modeled the costume. Or how many people it had taken to wrangle the dog into submission. She'd been trying for over half an hour to get the costume on the dog. He wasn't cooperating. Normally a very laid-back type of pooch, it appeared Charlie drew the line at dressing up for Halloween.

It had been two days since her date with Heath. She hadn't seen him since, but he'd texted and called, apologizing for not being able to see her in person and explaining that he'd had leave town to meet with new investors.

But he'd called a short while ago, said he was back and asked if he could stop by because he'd missed her. Jade held his words to her like a precious gift. He'd *missed* her. She'd confessed to missing him too.

After speaking with Heath, her package with Charlie's costume had been delivered, and Jade had thought she'd let him model the outfit for Heath. If she couldn't get the dog to wear the costume, never mind showing it off to Heath, what was she going to tell the kids? She'd promised them a fun Halloween parade at the zoo with Charlie as the parade marshal. The children all loved Charlie and were excited to see him in his special outfit.

"C'mon, Charlie, you don't want to disappoint all those kids, do you?"

The basset shook himself and backed away from her and the dreaded costume.

"I'll bet the kids will have so much fun they'll want to shower you with love and—" she looked him in the eye "—extra treats."

He perked up a bit at the word "treats," but then his gaze landed on the costume, and he backed up another step. Evidently the lure of dog biscuits wasn't enough to convince him to wear the outfit. Why hadn't she thought of Charlie refusing to cooperate when she promised the kids a dog costume parade?

Maybe her dad had been right. She didn't have whatever it took to be a success. At anything. She'd attended college but hadn't kept at it long enough to earn a degree. She'd tried her hand at several jobs, but most hadn't worked out either.

Maybe she—*No!* She was doing a good job with the petting zoo and running the day camps for the kids in town. And Heath had praised what she was doing, had said a similar program helped him. She may not ever be as rich or successful in business as her dad or Heath, but if she could help some other child reach his or her potential because of what she was doing, she'd call that a win. And she could live with that. She didn't think money was the only way to measure success.

She looked at Charlie and gave it one more try. "You get to be the grand marshal. That means you get to lead the parade. Wouldn't you like being the leader?"

"Not everyone is cut out to be a leader."

Jade twisted around at the sound of the familiar voice. Her heart skipped a beat when she saw Heath standing in the doorway of the barn belonging to the petting zoo. Seeing him made her realize how much she had missed him. And it had only been two days. Oh man, she was in trouble. She stood and smiled. "And you think Charlie is a born follower?"

Charlie ran over to Heath as if he were expecting salvation. Heath bent down and greeted the dog by rubbing his ears and running a hand over his long, squat body. The basset snuffled and squirmed in delight.

Dressed casually in worn jeans and a faded dark blue Henley with the sleeves pushed up to his elbows, Heath looked like every woman's dream. As if that wasn't enough, he also had on a pair of worn Ropers. The state of his boots told Jade that he was the real deal, not just some wannabe wearing the clothes. Something about that went straight to her heart.

And he was here to see her and had agreed to accompany her to the high school reunion. How lucky could she get? Even Nina and Alexis were envious. It didn't matter that she'd made up the whole engagement, Heath had backed her up, and they were forced to believe it.

He drew her attention away from her thoughts when he rose and hooked his thumbs into the front pockets of his jeans. "What is it you're trying to get him to do?"

Her cheeks grew warm. What if he laughed at her? "I need him to wear a costume in the Halloween parade I'm planning for the zoo. The parade and the party that follows it is the grand finale of all the Halloween Happenings I've got planned for the kids."

He raised his eyebrows. Although he didn't say anything, his expression was saying, *Are you freaking kidding me?*

"It's a cute dog costume." She looked at it. "And it cost me a pretty penny too." Jade held up the double-brimmed deerstalker cap and the brown houndstooth plaid trench coat trimmed with satin. The outfit was actually quite clever and well made. But along with Charlie not wanting to cooperate, she wondered if the kids had even heard of Sherlock Holmes.

Heath shook his head and looked at Charlie. "I gotta say, bud, I wouldn't be feeling it either. Costumes haven't been my thing in a long time."

"Oh great, encourage him, why don't you." She twisted her lips. If she was looking for an ally in this whole thing, it obviously wasn't Heath.

He rubbed a hand over his mouth and cleared his throat.

She knew he was hiding a smile, and she couldn't blame him. The whole thing *was* silly, but she still had an ace up her sleeve. "It's all for the kids. They'll be so disappointed. I know how much they've been looking forward to this."

He looked down at the dog and spread his hands and palms out in supplication. "What can I say, bud? It's for the kids."

Charlie whined and hung his head as if he understood but still didn't want to cooperate. The look he gave Heath said he felt like he'd been double-crossed.

"I feel you, Charlie, but sometimes we have to do things we don't want to please the people in our lives."

Jade's insides tightened. Was he talking about taking her to the reunion? Was he doing it simply to please her? Of course he was. It wasn't like he wanted to attend a function with a bunch of strangers.

You didn't think he really wanted to go with you? said a voice in her head that sounded suspiciously like Casper Windham.

She had to clear her throat before she could speak. "You don't have to go. It's okay. Really. I understand."

Heath's head snapped up; his eyes tight in the corners. "Are you talking to me or Charlie?"

"You." Now she felt miserable. She'd managed to convince herself he wanted to go with her. Not just to help her out but because maybe, just maybe, he enjoyed being in her company.

"Why do I get the feeling that I'm talking about dog parades and you're not?"

She swallowed. Hard. Was it possible that he really *was* referring to Charlie's refusal to put on the costume? She didn't want to create a whole misunderstanding by not getting clarity. "It's just that—"

He cut her off by covering her mouth with his.

His actions caught Jade off guard, but she soon melted against him. How could she not? The way his lips explored hers had her eyes threatening to roll back in her head. His actions may have been swift when he began the kiss, but now he was taking his time. *Savoring* was the only way to describe what his mouth was doing to hers.

The kiss was not some fantasy kiss; it was so much more. There was nothing sweet or gently seductive about it. The lip-lock was all about primal masculine desire and fiercely controlled passion. The kind of kiss a man gave a woman when he set out to make it clear he wanted her.

She knew there were only two possible responses to a kiss like that: she could return it with equal ardor or she could break free and step back. She doubted there was any middle ground. And in that moment, she knew she was *all in*. Wrapping her arms around his neck and kissing him back with a sensual hunger she'd never experienced, excitement sent adrenaline coursing through her.

By the time he freed her lips, she was hot and cold, breathless and a little shaky. She clutched him, savoring his scent and the hard feel of his unyielding body. When she kissed the warm skin of his throat, he exhaled deeply. Was it a sigh of pleasure, surrender or exaltation?

He used one finger to raise her chin, His mouth came back down on hers in another intense kiss. She could feel the heat of the fire that smoldered just beneath the surface.

She wanted the moment to go on indefinitely, but that wasn't realistic. And she had to keep reminding herself that this was a fake relationship even if the embrace was real. She knew guys didn't always have to have deep feelings for a woman in order to engage in a sexual relationship.

A loud braying bark spoiled the mood and Heath lifted his head. They stared at one another, each breathing heavily, for several moments before he stepped back.

Charlie lifted his head and howled.

"I think we're embarrassing Charlie," Heath said and contemplated the dog.

"Sorry about that. He's a very opinionated dog." Jade tried to keep the disappointment over the abrupt ending to that mind-blowing kiss out of her voice.

"It appears Charlie doesn't have one romantic bone in that low-slung body of his."

The dog hung his head as Heath squatted down and

picked up the costume. "How about we do a little nego-tiating? I'll bet you enjoy going for rides. Most dogs do."

"Next to treats and naps, it's his favorite thing," Jade chimed in.

"I have a proposition for you, Charlie, my man. Put the costume on, and I'll take you for a ride in my G Wagon. How does that sound?"

Jade took a step toward them. "Oh, I don't think that—"

Heath stopped her with a finger pressed to his lips and a shake of his head.

"Deal?" he asked the dog.

Charlie seemed to consider the idea, then sat down with a sigh. Heath took that as a yes and put the costume on him, including the deerstalker cap.

"Wait. Let me get some pictures." Jade pulled her cell phone out of her pocket and began snapping away. If Charlie refused to put the costume on again, at least she'd have something to show the kids. She made sure to get some with Heath in the photo too. Sort of a me-mento of that unforgettable kiss.

"What is he's supposed to be?" he asked.

She heaved a sigh reminiscent of Charlie's of a mo-ment ago. "He supposed to be Sherlock Hound."

Heath studied the dog. "Okay. I see it. Clever."

"No, it's not. If you didn't recognize the costume, there's no chance the kids will either. What was I *think-ing*?"

"Hey, don't give up. We can explain it to them."

Jade picked up on his use of the word "we" and felt better, but that didn't solve the problem of a cute but unrecognizable costume. "Wanna bet most of the kids have never heard of Sherlock Holmes?"

Heath gently rubbed his knuckles across her back. "Consider it a teachable moment."

"They're a little young for Sherlock."

He snapped his fingers. "But not too young for Encyclopedia Brown."

"Encyclopedia Brown? I remember loving those books. I enjoyed helping solve the mysteries and fancied myself being a girl detective."

Pulling out his phone, Heath said, "I saw you were giving out prizes to the kids. How many kids are you expecting?"

"I'm not totally sure yet." She hadn't gotten back all the signup sheets yet.

He waved his hand in a dismissive gesture as he studied his phone. "No matter. I'll order seventy-five copies. That should cover it. Any extras we can donate to the school."

"Any extras of what?"

"I just ordered sets of the Encyclopedia Brown series. I think the kids will enjoy them, and we can explain that Sherlock Holmes is also a detective, albeit an adult."

Leave it up to Heath to come up with a solution. "You're a real problem solver, Heath Blackwood. No wonder your company is so successful. How can I ever thank you?"

"No thanks needed, but I think we need to give Charlie his reward."

His tail wagging, the basset watched Heath.

"We can take my ranch truck. Not much can harm that old thing," Jade said.

Heath shook his head. "That wasn't the deal. Was it, buddy?"

The dog woofed in agreement.

"But...you may not realize this, but Charlie is a drool monster."

Heath brushed his mouth lightly against hers. "I've been around him enough to know he drools and sheds."

"And loves to roll around in the mud," she added.

He laughed. "Can't forget that."

Squatting down, he started to remove the costume and looked up at Jade. "Unless you'd rather I keep this on him?"

"No. Take it off. No telling what could happen to it if we leave it on." She gave him a wary look. "Are you *sure* you want to take your Mercedes for this ride?"

He chuckled and rubbed the dog's ears. "Positive. I have an important bit of business to conduct." After finishing his task, he stood and handed the folded costume to Jade, who put it on the workbench in the barn. She picked up the leash from the bench and clipped it to Charlie's collar. The dog barked and danced around, his tail wagging. "What sort of business? Where are we going?" she asked.

"We're going to the lake, by the dock. And it's important business," he said.

She gave him a narrow-eyed stare but decided to be patient. He seemed to be in a good mood, so she tried not to worry. She doubted he'd take her for a ride to the dock at the lake if he had some bad news, like he wouldn't be continuing their fake engagement.

"Important business?" she repeated.

"Very," he responded with an eyebrow wiggle and a wink.

That wink made her heart do all kinds of foolish things.

Chapter Seven

"Now, try to behave yourself in Heath's car," Jade told Charlie as they followed Heath to his Mercedes.

"I'm sure he'll be fine," Heath said over his shoulder, and opened the door to the back seat.

"What's that?" She pointed to the back seat.

"Oh. That?" he said with a wide grin.

"Yeah, that. It looks like an animal car seat, but you don't have a pet." Maybe he was thinking of getting one or had recently had one. She'd felt close to him since their date, but the fact was she didn't know as much about him as she thought. She actually knew very little of his life outside of Chatelaine.

"Not me personally, but I know someone who has a dog that means a great deal to her." His eyes held a certain gleam. "I did it for her."

Warmth flooded Jade's chest. Had she heard that right? "Don't tell me you got that for Charlie?"

"I did." He nodded and widened his grin. "I saw that you had one, so I decided to get one too."

"But…but you don't want Charlie riding in your car on a regular basis."

He gave her a puzzled frown. "Says who?"

"Me. His owner. You experienced firsthand what mayhem and destruction he can cause."

"If you're talking about our first date, I beg to differ. I think the evening turned out quite well."

"He ruined all your plans," she reminded him, but her protestations were getting old even to her.

Heath narrowed his eyes. "How do you figure that?"

"You had the evening arranged at a nice restaurant. I can't imagine that staying home and eating lasagna and sitting on the porch listening to the cicadas and watching for fireflies could compare to what you had in mind when you asked me out."

"The only plan that mattered was spending time with you. Considering that, I got exactly what I wanted from the evening, with the bonus of home-cooked meal."

"You did?" His words were making her insides go all gooey.

He captured her chin between his thumb and index finger. "I got to spend it with you, Jade, which was the only thing that mattered. And your mom makes great lasagna."

"It was a great evening for me too, and my mom does make great lasagna."

"Then Charlie didn't ruin anything at all. I think everything turned out the way it was supposed to. Maybe he's a lot smarter than you're giving him credit for."

"Perhaps you're right." Jade smiled at Heath. "Do we have any plans for this ride?"

"I haven't driven around the lake yet and I'd like to. I believe there's an open field near the boat dock. Charlie might like to explore. What do you say, bud, ready to go for that ride?"

Charlie barked and did a little dance, letting Heath know he was all in for this adventure.

A moment later, Heath picked up Charlie and put him in the special car seat, making sure he was secure.

"Did I do it right?" he asked, and moved aside so Jade could double-check it.

"It looks fine," she said and took a step back and bumped into Heath. "Sorry."

"I'm not." He steadied her and turned her in the circle of his arms.

Being in Heath's arms felt so natural, and when he leaned down and kissed her, she fell even more under his spell. The kiss was short, but to Jade, it felt like a promise. A promise of more to come.

He rested his forehead against hers and sighed. "Please tell me I'm not in this alone."

"You're not in this alone," she said in a breathless tone.

He gazed into her eyes. "That's good to know."

Charlie barked and they both laughed.

"I guess we'd better get going," Heath said and opened the passenger door to assist Jade into the seat.

He went around the hood of the vehicle and slipped into the driver's seat.

"You said you had some business," Jade reminded him as he started the finely tuned engine.

"I'll explain when we get to our destination."

They drove the short distance to the dock area of the lake, and he parked in the gravel lot. He lifted Charlie down from the SUV. The dog shook himself and tugged on the leash wanting to explore.

Meandering around the area, they followed the basset hound as he went from place to place and sniffed. They reached a small barbecue area, and Heath suggested they sit on one of the picnic benches.

Once seated, Heath reached into his pocket and pulled out a small box. A *jeweler's box*. The kind that held a ring.

Jade's breath caught in her throat. Why would he be giving her a ring? Despite the fevered kiss of a few moments ago, this was still a fake relationship. Attempting to remain calm and rational over this, she went over everything he'd said since he arrived.

He had told the dog he had business to take care of. Is this how he saw giving her the ring? As a piece of business? Because the engagement wasn't real.

Don't start fantasizing just because his kiss knocked you for a loop. He was a good kisser, and they might even have chemistry, but that didn't mean he saw this engagement as anything other than a face-saving favor.

He opened the box and showed her the ring nestled inside. The white gold ring had a sapphire in a prong setting. The round cut enhanced the gemstone's natural sparkle and color. She gasped at the beauty of it. "I couldn't possibly accept something like this."

"Why not? Don't you like sapphires?" He sounded surprised by her refusal.

"Of course I like it. What's not to like? It's a gorgeous ring." Its magnificence had everything to do with her decision. How could she in good conscience accept jewelry knowing their relationship wasn't real? Why was he even offering it to her?

"Then what is the problem?" he asked, his jaw tightening.

Her heart sank. Insulting him was the last thing she wanted to do. "It must have cost a fortune. I can't accept such an extravagant gift under false pretenses."

He frowned. "False pretenses?"

"You said yourself you can't be in a serious relationship with anyone until the mystery of your birth is solved." She needed to get ahead of this and explain her side.

"And your point is?"

"To be perfectly honest, this looks like a serious ring."

"It might look like it, but believe me, it's not." He shook his head. "I think it would be a good idea to wear it for the reunion. Help sell our story to your classmates."

His explanation sounded logical, but did they really need help selling their story? "I'm no expert in jewelry, but I know sapphires can be pricey."

"Not all of them."

She'd take his word for it. What else could she do? "Was there a reason you picked a sapphire?"

"It's supposed to be a perfect gemstone for hazel eyes."

Her heart thudded. He'd picked out a ring because of her eye color? She'd bet some of the guys she'd known would have been hard-pressed to even remember her eye color.

"I promise to take good care of it. I'm sure you'll want it back after…after…" The thought of their fake engagement coming to an end made her queasy.

Get used to it, she cautioned herself. This isn't real. None of this is real.

"Let's not worry about that."

"Okay," she agreed. She was most certainly setting herself up for heartache in the future. But the keyword here was *future*, and she decided today wasn't a good day to worry about it. She'd enjoy being with Heath, and if today was all she was getting, then so be it.

Heath wanted to give himself a good kick. That didn't go *at all* like he'd planned. He'd assumed Jade would have jumped at the chance for a ring like that. He'd probably have to explain it as part of their engagement story, but then he'd offer it and she'd accept. End of story. But Jade was different, and that's why he was having trouble remembering that this whole thing was temporary. He'd take her to her reunion and then what?

Maybe he'd solve the mystery surrounding his birth father before the reunion, and he could get on with his life, depending on what answers he'd receive.

"So, you'll wear the ring…for now at least?" The truth was, he wanted her to have it. As for why, he hadn't a clue. He didn't understand his own reasoning, so how was he expected to explain it to her?

"If you want me to, I will." Her tone was solemn, as if she were making a vow.

Was she making a vow? He pushed that thought aside, just as he had the crazy notion of going down on one knee before giving Jade the sapphire ring.

Instead of kneeling, he gently took her left hand in his and slowly slipped the ring onto her finger. He squeezed her fingers as he seated the ring in place. It looked right, as if it truly belonged on her finger. As if she truly belonged to him. The thought made his heart stutter.

He led her over to a picnic table so they could sit and watch the dog.

"Charlie looks like he's running out of steam," he said.

The dog had been running around the grassy area but had taken to lying under a tree.

"Yeah, he's not known for his endurance. He likes to run around for short bursts, but then he's ready for a nap," Jade said with a chuckle.

"That's a good philosophy to embrace," Heath said and got the reaction he'd been going for. Jade laughed. God, how he loved that laugh.

They bundled Charlie back into the car. Securing the dog into the special animal car seat made him think about what it would be like to have a family of his own. A family with Jade. Did she even want kids? Did he? How could he bring a child into the world until he knew the secret behind his birth story?

They got into the SUV, and he pulled out onto the road leading back to the Fortune ranch.

"What made you pick this model of car?" she asked curiously.

He glanced at her for a second before turning his attention back on the road. "Pardon? What do you mean?"

"I just wondered what drew you to it."

He shrugged. "I liked it."

"Fair enough."

Was she simply making conversation? "Why? What's your dream car?"

"Promise not to laugh?" she asked.

He felt her gaze on him. "Promise."

"It *was* a Maserati Quattroporte."

"Was?"

She had made him promise not to laugh, but then she did so herself. "It sounded so exotic to me, then I found out Quattroporte just means four—"

"Doors," he finished for her. He managed not to laugh but couldn't prevent the smile that curled his lips.

"See. You're making fun of me. It lost some of its luster when I learned the mundane English translation."

"I most certainly am not making fun. As a matter of fact, you have great taste in luxury cars." He knew Casper Windham had been worth a lot of money, so Jade and her family had never been poor. Not like he and his mom. But despite the privileged upbringing, Jade was very down to earth. Which is what had drawn him to her in the first place.

"Yeah, well, I couldn't have one with Charlie." She heaved a sigh.

"Why? Does he object to Italian luxury cars?"

She laughed. "No, but he'd want to go every time I drove anywhere, and you've seen how much he drools."

He waved a hand. "You worry too much about that."

"But you keep your car so clean."

"I like to take care of the things I have. I didn't have a lot growing up and take care of the things I have now in my life."

"You appreciate them," she said softly.

"I guess you could say that. I don't like to take anything for granted."

"You started the Anne Blackwood Foundation to help disadvantaged kids stay in school and get a higher education."

"How did you find out about that? I don't publicize it." Heath didn't do it for the kudos. He'd simply seen a need and decided to fulfill it. The project helped him honor the legacy his mother had given him. He wasn't able to help her now that he was rich, but he could help others in her name.

"You've been googling me?"

She shrugged but didn't deny it. "Why don't you like to take credit for it?"

"I don't deny its existence, but I don't need accolades to accomplish what I want."

"I admire you for that. You're nothing like my father was."

"And that's a good thing?" he asked but was pretty sure he knew the answer. He noticed Jade was not comfortable talking about her father.

"A very good thing," she said, but didn't elaborate.

Her words gave him conflicting feelings. He was glad she admired the things he'd accomplished, but it also made him wonder how she'd feel if he discovered negative reasons why James Perry had never acknowledged him.

Jade held out her left hand and admired the sapphire ring. She'd been doing that ever since Heath had given it to her.

After he'd left yesterday, she'd told herself she would wear it to the reunion and only then. Her family knew the truth, so there was no need to pretend in front of them.

At least that had been the plan, but she'd been unable to bring herself to take the beautiful ring off. Every time she started to remove it, she heard Heath saying he'd picked a sapphire to complement her hazel eyes.

"Jade? I saw your message and thought I'd come and check on the lamb."

Jade turned at the sound of her sister's voice. Dahlia was walking across the grass toward the barn.

Glancing at her left hand and the ring, she grimaced. Too late to remove the ring without calling attention to it.

"How is he doing?"

"Yesterday he was disappointed after speaking with—" Jade broke off abruptly. She had to assume her face was probably a nice candy apple red by now. Of course Dahlia had meant the lamb, but Jade's mind was so full of Heath that she'd answered automatically.

"Oh, wow! He speaks? That'll be a big draw for the petting zoo." Dahlia was obviously working hard to keep a straight face.

"Ha ha. I was talking about—"

"Heath Blackwood," her sister said without trying to hide her grin. "I was going to inquire about him next, but we can start with him first if you'd like."

"We'll talk about the lamb and only the lamb, if you don't mind."

Dahlia raised an eyebrow. "And if I *do* mind?"

Jade rolled her eyes at her younger sister's antics and briefly wondered if Heath teased or got teased by his sisters. Had their relationship evolved to that point? Did meeting your sibling as an adult change that dynamic? They might—

"So, about the lamb?"

Dahlia's question chased away Jade's musings over Heath. *Get out of your head, Jade.*

"The lamb is doing much better since I removed him from the petting area."

"What was the problem? Did one of the kids do something?"

Jade shook her head. "No. I think he found all the attention from humans stressful, so I moved him to the barn."

Dahlia made a face. "The poor thing. First his mama rejects him and now this."

Jade patted her sister's shoulder. "Don't fret. He's been befriended by one of the baby goats, and I'm keeping them together. They're both doing much better, but I may not be able to keep them as part of the actual petting zoo. But don't worry, I will look after them regardless of that."

"You're such a soft touch with the animals. I think you've found your true calling, Sis."

"I'm grateful to the family for this opportunity."

Dahlia smiled over at her sister. "We're grateful to you for taking it over and making a success of both the zoo and the children's workshops in such a short time and—"

Jade glanced at Dahlia, wondering what made her stop.

"Oh my God, Jade, where'd you get that sapphire?

That's some *serious bling*." Dahlia grabbed Jade's left hand to get a closer look at the ring. "It looks like an engagement ring. Jade? Are you holding out on us?"

Jade pulled her hand out of Dahlia's grasp. "What do you mean? It's just part of the fake engagement story, not a real engagement ring."

"It might not be a real engagement, but that ring is the real deal."

"Well, of course it's real. I'm wearing it, aren't I?" Jade told her sister, but she started to get an uncomfortable feeling in the pit of her stomach. Those weren't butterflies swarming in there but bats. Enough bats to make the citizens of Austin envious.

"I'm not a jeweler, but that ring didn't come from a cereal box."

Was it possible that Heath bought a real ring for her to wear? Real, as in expensive? Of course he was wealthy, but he didn't seem like the type to throw his money around. The only thing flashy about him was his car, and even that wasn't all that flashy. She'd seen plenty of soccer moms driving G Wagons at the country club.

"I think this guy is serious," her sister said.

"Really?" Damn, she wanted to kick herself for sounding so needy.

"And why not?"

"I'm not exactly the type of woman a billionaire picks."

Her sister narrowed her eyes. "What's that supposed to mean?"

"Rich, successful men want beauty queens on their arms," Jade said, repeating something Casper had said to her on more than one occasion. In the past, Jade hadn't cared because she didn't want a rich, successful man. And now?

"That's bull crap."

"No, that's Casper Windham."

Her sister put her arm around her. "I know Daddy did a number on you, but he was wrong. Dead wrong. About a lot of things but especially about you, Jade. Look what you've done with this place."

"The zoo didn't have any animals left, but the buildings and such were already here."

"Don't undercut all you've accomplished," Dahlia admonished her. "You've done a wonderful job."

"I renovated the place and brought it up to date with a lot of help from others," Jade said, but her sister's praise gave her a warmth that spread across her chest.

"You've given it *heart*. But enough about the zoo. Let's talk about that ring."

Jade looked down at the dazzling sapphire. "You're sure it's real?"

"Positive, and I'm positive about what I see when Heath looks at you."

Even after Dahlia had left, Jade couldn't stop thinking about what her sister said about Heath. Was it possible that he was falling for her as hard as she was falling for him?

Chapter Eight

Heath stepped inside Fortune's Castle after returning from a meeting with investors in Houston. He loosened his tie as he strolled inside and crossed the grand entryway with its black-and-white checkerboard floor tiles. As always, he glanced up at the elaborate wrought-iron candelabra hung from the ceiling painted with a Byzantine-style mosaic of peacocks and birds.

Would he ever not be taken aback by the opulence of the place, he wondered, shaking his head at the black torch-shaped sconces interspersed with paintings of medieval lords and ladies in outdoor landscapes lined one wall.

It felt good to be home. His last thought caused him to stumble, but he caught himself before falling and embarrassing himself.

When had he started thinking of Chatelaine as home? When he'd first arrived, he planned on staying only long enough to meet with his newly discovered sisters and to find answers to the questions surrounding James Perry. But those plans had started to morph once he met Jade Fortune and agreed to be her fake fiancé for her reunion.

He had a feeling that Jade had a lot to do with his thinking of Chatelaine as home.

The hotel might not be fully operational yet, but staff had been hired and were obviously being trained. He halted as a group of trainees followed a member of management through the lobby. He glanced over at the reception counter and the desk clerk waved at him.

The woman, who appeared to be in her mid to late twenties, also called out. "Mr. Blackwood, sir?"

He changed direction and went to the counter instead of the bank of elevators. "Something wrong?"

The woman gave him an engaging smile. "No, sir. I found this on the counter when I came back from getting some copy paper from the back room."

She held up a plain white envelope with his name printed in shaky block letters.

"Do you know who left it for me?" he asked. This was all very odd, but he did have to admit that the entire population of Chatelaine probably knew he was staying at the Castle even if it wasn't formally open.

"Not a clue. I'm sorry, but our security cameras aren't hooked up yet. But it must be someone who knows you're staying here."

He took the envelope and grunted. "I'm sure that's the entire town."

She laughed. "Pretty much. Not many secrets in Chatelaine. That's for sure."

Except for the mystery surrounding the circumstances of his birth. Why he never knew his father, and his mother felt the need to keep it a secret. He should have pursued it more forcefully with Anne. He would have if he'd had any inkling that she would have been gone so soon and so quickly. The cancer that took her had worked fast. He'd tried to press her a few times, but when he saw how agitated the subject made her, he backed off. So that was on him. But truly, how could he hound a dying woman? And he didn't want her to think she hadn't been enough. She'd asked him that once when he'd prodded her for details on his father. After that, he'd let it go. And the information she'd had was buried with her.

He appreciated that she hadn't had an easy time of raising him as a single mother but he had never lacked for love. They may not have had a lot of luxuries but she saw that he always had the basics. He missed her and wished he could've had more time to spoil her once he started making large sums of money.

"Is there a problem, sir? As I said, the envelope was here when I got back from my errand."

The desk clerk's question pulled him out of his morose thoughts, and he gave her a vague smile. "No problem at all." After a quick glance at her name tag, he added, "Thanks again, Sara."

He glanced at the envelope as he walked toward the elevator. Strange. Despite his curiosity, he decided to wait until he reached his room to open it. No telling what it contained.

Once inside his suite, he dropped his briefcase on the desk and tore open the envelope. There was a single sheet of paper inside. It was plain white copy paper. On it was a handwritten note in the same shaky block letters.

Your mother was deeply in love with James Perry,
but he did her dirty.

Heath turned the note over, but it was blank. The note
was also unsigned. Had it come from Doris Edwards?
She had said something similar when Heath had gone
to see her for the first time with his sisters.

He debated with himself for a minute but decided not
to tell the triplets about the note. He didn't want to taint
whatever they thought of their father. They might have
been too young for any personal memories of him, but
people had shared their memories with the girls, and he
wasn't going to mess with that. Besides, he didn't know
the whole story.

Would going to see Doris again help? He remembered
how she'd ended up rambling the last time. He wasn't
sure he was interested in engaging in that frustrating
exercise again. Maybe at some point he would, but not
at the moment.

According to the note, his mother had been in love
with his father. Was that a good thing or not? Heath
wasn't sure. Had James Perry truly taken advantage of
his mother? Or had she just fallen for the wrong man?
Considering how close in age he was to his half sisters,
a mere two months, had he led two women on? Obviously James had married his sisters' mother. What about
Anne? Had he simply dropped her despite her being
pregnant? Or maybe his time with his mother had been
an extramarital affair. Was James the kind of man who
found it impossible to be faithful? Heath knew the type

but, despite having James Perry's blood and DNA, didn't think he could be that cruel as to cheat on a spouse.

And if James *had* cheated with Heath's mother, how would his sisters feel about that? Would they somehow feel Heath's mother was responsible for the way their father treated their mother?

Now that he'd found his siblings, Heath did not want to sever the bond that was being forged between them. Maybe he shouldn't even be *on* this quest. He would have to share his results at some point, but the last thing he wanted to do was hurt Haley, Lily or Tabitha.

He decided to change out of his business clothes and go to see the one person who might help him make sense of this. She made everything in his life feel different.

"What is it you're doing?"

Jade's stomach somersaulted at the sound of his voice. She'd set up a table in the doorway of the largest barn at the petting zoo so she could work on her craft project for Halloween Happenings. She set down the pair of pliers in her hand and drank in the sight of Heath. Today he was wearing faded jeans, a denim work shirt and a pair of scuffed black Ropers. A tingle ran along her spine. This feeling was becoming a habit whenever she was with him. Would it always be like this? Or would she get used to being with him?

Get used to being with him?

Where did that thought even come from? Theirs wasn't a real relationship. Heath was doing her a favor by not telling everyone how she'd lied about their engagement.

Heath stood next to a sawhorse, and an image of him astride a horse came unbidden into her mind, threatening to leave her breathless.

"Do you ride?" she blurted out before she could stop herself. He was going to be convinced she didn't know how to carry on an intelligent conversation if she kept asking him outlandish questions.

"Depends on what you're talking about riding."

Warmth bloomed in her cheeks, and she could only pray that she didn't resemble a ripe tomato. "Horses."

"Yes," he said, drawing the word out so it had three syllables.

"Why am I sensing a 'but' in there?"

"Maybe because that's what gets sore when I ride," he said, his lips twitching.

"I meant the *but* with only one *t*, but I guess you answered my question." She laughed. At least he wasn't calling her names for inciting inane conversations, like the one about the English translation of Quattroporte. "So am I to understand you don't like horseback riding?"

"Depends on who I'm riding with. If you're asking, then I'm willing."

"Sore butt and all?" She'd have to check with Nash or Ridge and perhaps they could arrange a riding date.

"I figure it would be worth it. When did you have in mind?"

She wasn't about to tell him that the whole thing stemmed from a vision she'd had of him as a cowboy astride a horse. "I didn't have any specific time in mind. I was just curious. After all, this is a ranch, so I'm sure we can scare up some horses."

"Let me know when and where, and I'll be there." He squatted on his haunches next to her Halloween project. "Now, what is this going to be?"

"It's something I saw online and thought it would be great for the costume party and parade I have planned for the kids." She pulled out her phone and searched for what had given her the inspiration.

She found it and handed him the phone. He took it from her, and when he did, his fingers brushed against hers. Again with the tingles from the skin-to-skin contact.

"Very clever."

"I thought so."

Then Jade showed him what she was doing with the tomato cages. She'd turned them upside down and twisted the bottom spikes together and tied them. Using a Styrofoam ball, she stuck it onto the gather spikes. Then she wound a string of clear lights around the cage. She covered the entire thing with a precut square of white cloth.

"Whadaya think?" She sat back and checked out her creation.

"I think it needs some eyes."

"That's right! I almost forgot." She checked the bag of supplies she'd brought with her and pulled out two circles cut from black felt. "I'll need to glue them on."

"Can I do it?"

"Sure." She handed him the felt circles and the fabric glue she'd picked up at GreatStore, along with the other supplies to make the ghosts.

"We'll need to plug them in," he said as he put the cap back on the glue.

"I brought some power strips and extension cords." She pointed to the plastic bags stacked against the side of the barn.

"How many did you plan on making?"

"I'm not sure yet. I decided to try this one first and see how it came out before I committed myself to half a dozen."

He nodded. "Let me get this one hooked up so you can see how it looks."

She watched him walk into the barn and couldn't help but admire him. Tall, loose-limbed and totally delicious. And he was all hers.

What? No, no, no.

Get that thought out of your head right now, Jade Fortune. This is all make believe. Your feelings might be real, but the situation isn't.

"So, how does it look?" Heath asked as he came back out of the barn.

"What?"

"Your ghost. How does it look?" He gave her a scrutinizing look.

How could she have forgotten the ghost? She studied her creation with a critical eye but had to admit it looked pretty good.

This is what you need to concentrate on, she told herself. Forget building make-believe castles and fairy tales.

Heath watched Jade closely. Before he entered the barn to plug in the extension cord, she'd been excited about her project. He saw it in the gleam in her eyes, the glow on her cheeks. He could have planned his future on that smile and the soft expression in those hazel eyes. But when he emerged from the barn, she had changed. As if a switch had been flipped. She was still smiling, but he detected something different. It didn't light up her eyes as it had before. He sighed, thinking how in tune he was to her various moods. Not a good sign if he expected to walk away from this phony relationship with his heart intact.

"The kids are going to get a kick out of them." She came to stand beside him. "What do you think?"

Jade's scent filled his senses with a combination of soap, shampoo and what he suspected was laundry detergent or fabric softener. She didn't need cloying perfume to smell good or to catch his eye. Everything about her grabbed his attention from the moment he'd spotted her leaving the Daily Grind as he drove through Chatelaine for the first time. Maybe that's why the coffee shop had become a favorite—

"Heath?"

"What?" He pushed his thoughts aside. "Sorry. What did you say?"

She gave him a speculative glance. "I asked what you thought of my ghost."

"I love it, and I'm sure the kids will too."

She nodded. "Thanks. I agree. I'll use up the rest of the supplies and make some more."

"Would you like some help?" He had assembled the prototypes for his drone and laser weed zappers and was pretty sure he could handle some tomato cage ghosts.

"I'd love it. Thanks." She glanced at him with an

unreadable expression. "You're sure you don't mind? I know how busy you are."

"Not too busy to help you," he told her, then added, "Like we told Charlie, it's for the kids."

"Right. For the kids," she said in a monotone.

Great. Why did he have to tack on that last bit? Yes, part of him was doing it for the children, but a very small part. Mostly he was doing it because of Jade.

She'd begun assembling another ghost, so he chose supplies to make his own.

"How was your trip to Houston? Did you accomplish what you set out to do?" she asked as she wound lights around the tomato cage.

"I think so. The investors are definitely interested," he said, but his thoughts while there had been on what waited for him upon his return.

"But?"

He looked up from his partially finished ghost. "There was a strange letter waiting for me at the hotel."

"A notice from the management?"

"No. It was an anonymous note. It said, and I quote, 'Your mother was deeply in love with James Perry, but he did her dirty.'"

Heath stuck the Styrofoam ball onto the spike ends of the tomato cage. Stepping back, he checked to be sure he hadn't damaged the Styrofoam. He'd used a bit more force than had been necessary. Thank goodness his rough treatment hadn't harmed anything.

"Oh, wow. That is disturbing. Any clue who sent it. Was there a postmark?"

He began stringing the tiny lights around the structure. "It wasn't sent through the mail. The desk clerk at the hotel said she found it on the counter addressed to me. She didn't see who dropped it off, and their security cameras aren't hooked up yet."

"Do you think Doris Edwards wrote it?"

"That was my first thought, but I don't know how she would have delivered it to Fortune's Castle."

Jade shrugged. "She could have had someone give her a ride or got someone else to bring it. My mother has begun employing a lot of locals so someone could have dropped off the note for her."

"I guess it doesn't matter how it got to me. The fact is it did." He finished wrapping the lights and made sure they were secure.

"And its contents are bothering you?"

"Yeah." He exhaled loudly. "Plus, I hate having to keep something from my sisters."

"Why would you feel the need to hide it from them?"

"It doesn't exactly paint James in a very good light. I hate to be the one giving them sketchy information about their biological father. Who says the note is even right?" He'd always been afraid his mother was the villain in the story, but the note made it sound like *she* was the victim.

"But the truth is exactly that...the truth. That note may be nothing but a lie, but whatever you find out, you can't protect them from the truth."

He nodded mutely, letting her words sink in.

"I'm sure they understand that whatever you find out about James Perry and his relationship with your mother doesn't affect your relationship with them," she added.

"Are you sure about that?"

"Not one hundred percent, but I didn't have a great relationship with my father while some of my siblings had a much better one with him. I don't hold that against them." Jade shrugged. "How could I? It wasn't their fault the way Casper treated me. And it's not your fault, or theirs, the way James treated your mother. Your sisters are smart, they'll understand that too."

As usual Jade knew how to make him feel better, and he trusted her judgment.

Ignoring his common sense and following his instincts, he moved toward her. Putting his hands on her slender shoulders, he pulled her to him and brought his mouth down on hers. Although his actions had been abrupt, he soon gentled his kiss, exploring her mouth with his. He drew the tip of his tongue across the seam of her lips, and she opened for him. His tongue slipped past her teeth to slide against hers.

An alarm sounded in his brain, and he took a step back. Not because he wanted to put distance between them. He did it because he *had* to. The situation was starting to get out of hand.

He should probably explain why he pulled away but wasn't sure he could. Instead, he waited a moment for his insides to settle back into place and for some oxygen to return to his brain.

"I, uh..." He blew out his breath.

She was breathing heavily. "Yeah. Me too."

"So I'm not in this alone?"

She shook her head.

"That's...reassuring."

She blew out a breath and laughed. "Yeah. It is."

"Maybe we should work on finishing these ghosts." He hitched his chin toward the table scattered with supplies.

"Good idea." She got back to work on the half-finished ghost. Clearing her throat, she asked, "Does the fact that I'm older than you bother you?"

"You're older than me?" He placed a hand across his chest in a theatrical gesture. Her age didn't bother him, but he wasn't entirely sure how she felt.

"Yes. You must have realized it when—you're teasing me."

"Now, Jade, this is hardly a matter for levity. I'm involved with an older woman. That's rather shocking, don't you think?" he asked, trying his best to keep a straight face.

"You ought to get together with my sister Dahlia," she muttered.

"Well, she is younger than you, but I have a feeling that her husband Rawlston might not take too kindly to that." He'd heard that Dahlia and Rawlston's marriage had had a rocky start, but everyone in Chatelaine agrees the couple is deeply in love. Nothing and no one were coming between those two.

"Very funny." Jade narrowed her eyes at him, but her lips twitched as if fighting a grin.

"I'm not so sure this is a laughing matter. I'm assuming Dahlia agrees with me about this troubling turn of events." He couldn't remember the last time, if ever, he'd teased a woman. He liked it. His whole relationship with Jade was different than any other.

Maybe because it's not real, a voice in his head

taunted, but he pushed it aside. The engagement might be fake but this moment with Jade was real—*she* was real—and he was going to enjoy it.

"Are you sure it doesn't bother you?"

"Cross my heart," he said.

"I—"

He cut her off by placing two fingers across her lips. "Not another word. Ever since I had a crush on my second grade teacher, I have had this thing for older women."

"You had a crush on your second grade teacher?" she asked.

"I don't remember much except she had long blond hair and wore red high heels."

"Wow. That's specific."

He laughed, shaking his head at the memory. "About the only thing I remember about second grade."

She laughed too. Boy did he love that sound. It was getting harder and harder to remember that this relationship was temporary.

But it had to be until he was able to solve the mystery surrounding James and Anne's history.

After Heath left, Jade called the school to let them know that Heath would be teaching the next workshop, which happened to be the following day. The school staff was excited and asked if they could send more than one grade to the ranch.

Heath, true to his word, arrived at about the same time as the school kids and their teachers. Also arriving were what appeared to be an abundance of parent chaperones, mostly mothers. Looked like the kids weren't the only ones excited by Heath's appearance. Not that Jade could blame them. The day was sunny and crisp, a perfect autumn morning. It was as if even the weather wanted to cooperate for Heath's demonstration.

Jade watched the children file obediently into the bleachers that had been set up several months ago for the workshops.

The only one not cooperating was Billy Connor. The boy and his mother had visited the petting zoo many times before. Jade knew how much he loved the zoo and the day camps he'd come to. The boy's teacher, Mrs. Miller, had taken him aside, so Jade sauntered over.

"I'm not sure what's wrong," Mrs. Miller confided to Jade, "but he's lost his chance to see the animals today," she said in a voice loud enough for Billy to hear.

Jade tried to get him to talk to her, but he shrugged his shoulders and hung his head. She did notice he was paying close attention to everything Heath said.

After the workshop and the drone demonstration, the kids, all except for Billy, raced off to see the animals at the petting zoo. The chaperones followed closely behind, but a few of the women glanced back at Heath. Jade couldn't blame them. Not one bit.

Heath nodded to Jade and headed over to where she stood with Billy and his teacher.

"Do you know Mr. Blackwood?" Billy tilted his head to look at Jade.

"As a matter of fact, I do," Jade told him and grinned when Billy said, "Cool."

Heath approached, glancing at Billy, who was busy

trying not to look awestruck, and raised his eyebrows in inquiry.

Mrs. Miller reached out her hand to the boy. "Billy, thank Mr. Blackwood for today's lesson, and then you come with me and give him and Miss Jade some privacy."

Warmth crept into Jade's cheeks. Evidently Billy's teacher had heard the gossip that was racing around town.

Billy thanked Heath and rippled with excitement when Heath reached out and shook his hand.

"You can go hang out with Charlie if that's okay with your teacher," Jade suggested and motioned with her head when the teacher nodded. "He's in the barn. He's in time-out today too."

"Dogs get time-out too?" Billy asked, his eyes wide.

"When they misbehave, they do," Jade told him.

Mrs. Miller took Billy by the hand and led him into the large red barn.

Heath glanced around, and with no one in sight, he leaned down and gave her a quick kiss. It was over almost before it began, but Jade still felt a tingle race down her spine at the contact.

"So, what's the deal with Billy?" Heath asked.

"He misbehaved on the bus over here and lost his petting zoo privileges. He was always such a good kid, but lately not so much. His mom and his teacher have both spoken with me about his behavior." Jade sighed. "I know how much he loves coming here. He's interested in the animals at the petting zoo. He even mentioned one time that he might want to be a veterinarian. I don't understand the change in him."

Heath's brows dipped toward the bridge of his nose. "I hate to hear that."

"I don't know what's wrong, but I could see he was paying attention to everything you said and did," Jade said and paused. Was she really going to do this? "He looks up to you. Maybe you can find out what's bothering him, and we can take it from there."

He seemed to consider it.

Jade shook her head and touched his arm. "I'm sorry. I shouldn't have put this on you. Forget that I even asked. This is above and beyond anything I should expect from you."

Heath put a hand on her shoulder and gently squeezed. "No. I want to help. He was curious about the drone. I'll offer to give him a closer look and maybe he'll open up."

"Thank you. And please, if he's not forthcoming, don't worry about it."

"I'll see what I can do."

Jade's heart skipped a beat as Heath sauntered over to where Billy was squatting down, talking to Charlie. Even if he couldn't find out what was bothering Billy, at least he was trying. More proof that Heath might be rich, successful and driven like Casper Windham had been, but that's where the similarities ended. He had proved time and time again that he cared about more than his business or making more money. Of course, that knowledge made her admire him even more. If she wasn't careful, she could end up falling in love with him. She shook her head, determined not to let that happen if she could help it. But the question was, could she help it?

Maybe you're more than a little in love already, a voice whispered in her head.

Heath had offered to help Jade put out juice boxes and cookies for the kids, but she'd shooed him away, saying she could handle it. He assumed she'd done that so he could use the opportunity to approach Billy. Normally, he wouldn't get involved, but he couldn't say no to Jade. And if she thought he could help, he'd at least give it a shot, although he didn't expect the kid to actually talk to him about anything personal.

Now, he stood next Billy, who was petting Charlie. The dog wagged his tail and greeted Heath like a long-lost friend.

"Hey, Mr. Blackwood, Charlie knows you," Billy said.

"He seems to know you too."

"Yeah, me and my mom love to come to Miss Jade's zoo," the boy told him.

The teacher smiled at Heath. He nodded at her unspoken question, and she said, "I'll go over and help Jade while you talk to Mr. Blackwood, but you have to promise to behave, Billy."

"I will. I promise." Billy said and stuck his chest out. "I really like your drone. Maybe someday I can do stuff like you and get to use one."

"Would you like me to show you up close how I use it?" Heath saw how fascinated Billy.

Billy's eyes were the size of saucers. "You mean it, Mr. Heath? You're gonna show me how to work the controls of the drone?"

"Yes, but you have to be very careful. It's not a toy."

"Oh, I'll be real careful. I promise."

Heath demonstrated how the controls worked and let Billy try it. "Miss Jade tells me you haven't been behaving yourself during her workshops lately."

"I'm sorry. My mom made me apologize to her already. Do I need to do it again?" The boy's lower lip trembled a bit, but he squared his shoulders.

"No, I don't think that's necessary, but I hope you will listen to her in the future. You know I got my start at workshops like the ones Miss Jade gives."

"Huh? What did you start?" Billy scrunched up his face.

Heath chuckled. "I started my company. I got lots of good ideas at those workshops, but that's because I paid attention."

"I promise to pay attention from now on."

"That's good. I think you disappoint others when you don't behave."

"I know but…" The boy hung his head.

"But what?" Heath asked gently but continued to show him how to work the controls rather than confront him directly. He wasn't sure if that method would work, but it was worth a shot.

"I dunno," Billy said and shrugged. "Do you have a dad?"

"Not really. My father died when I was a baby." If James Perry had truly been his father and must have been because DNA didn't lie. Not like people.

Heath's answer seemed to have caught Billy's attention. "So, like, you didn't know him at all?"

"No. I never met him." Heath didn't realize how much it would hurt to admit that.

"My dad died a couple years ago when I was little." Billy kicked his foot in the dirt. "But I can't remember what he sounds like anymore. Does that mean I'm gonna forget all the other stuff about him too?"

"Even if you forget some things about him, he'll always be here." Heath tapped Billy's chest. "He'll be in your heart."

"I guess. Is your dad in your heart even if you didn't meet him?"

Heath thought about it for a moment. "Yeah, I guess maybe he is."

Once the boy rejoined the group, Heath was able to let Jade know what had been bothering Billy. She said she'd be sure to speak with Mrs. Miller, who in turn could discuss it with the boy's mother.

Long after the kids had left, Heath thought about his talk with Billy and his answer to the kid's question. He carried James Perry's DNA, but what else did he carry? Had James really done Heath's mother dirty, or was there another explanation for what happened?

He really needed to find out the truth before he could form a meaningful relationship with Jade. It was only fair.

Chapter Nine

Jade had put this meeting off for as long as she could. She would have loved to delay it indefinitely, but she knew that wasn't going to happen, so she may as well get it over with. Her mother, as well as her sisters, wanted to take her shopping before the reunion. They would be taking the opportunity to give Jade a makeover.

Didn't they understand that she'd never be glamorous like the three of them?

She walked into the Cowgirl Café and immediately spotted her mother and two sisters in a booth. Wendy had extended the invitation, but Jade was pretty sure her mom had recruited Dahlia and Sabrina as reinforcements. Jade huffed out a breath. The way her mother and sisters were acting, you'd think she'd been invited to attend Cinderella's ball. If not for the debacle with Alexis and Nina, she wouldn't even be going.

Yes, the reunion was being held at a swanky country club and, considering most of the students came from well-to-do families, it would be a classy affair. But it hardly merited the battle plan that Wendy Fortune was sure to propose.

Jade had the urge to leave, but they had already spotted her, and her mom was waving her over.

"You made it." Wendy looked relieved to see Jade.

"I told you I was coming," she said as she slipped into the booth next to Sabrina.

"She was afraid you'd come up with an excuse to cancel at the last minute," Dahlia told her, picking up her coffee and blowing on the steaming brew. She cautiously took a sip.

"Dahlia, please," Wendy frowned at her daughter.

"What? It's the truth." Dahlia set her coffee mug down. "We know Jade doesn't like all the fuss."

Hannah, the waitress, appeared next to the booth. "Hey, Jade. Can I get you some coffee while you decide?"

"Yes, please, and I don't even have to check the menu. I'll have French toast and bacon."

Hannah stuck her order pad into the pocket of her white apron. "Extra crispy on the bacon?"

"You got it." One of the benefits of living in a small town. The waitresses knew what you liked to eat.

"Heard you and Heath Blackwood are gonna tie the knot." Hannah paused before walking away to place Jade's order. "That true?"

And that was the *downside* of living in a small town. Everyone not only knew your business, or thought they did, and weren't shy to ask all about it.

Jade unfolded her napkin and set the silverware next to it. "We haven't made any official announcements yet."

The waitress nodded. "Well, let me add my congratulations. You two make a cute couple. Be right back with the coffee."

Jade watched her walk away, her words ringing in her ears. She hadn't really thought about how people saw them as a couple.

"It's true," Wendy said and picked up her own coffee mug. "You do make a cute couple."

"But you know the truth," Jade told her mother. She didn't need her family to believe in this fake engagement because she might start buying into it herself.

"I'm so glad you're letting us help you get ready for this party," Wendy said, strategically changing the subject.

Or willingly ignoring it. Jade wasn't sure which and wasn't sure what she preferred. But changing the subject was for the best. As much as she didn't want to discuss what to wear to the reunion, she wanted to dissect her complicated nonrelationship with Heath even less.

Wendy patted Jade's hand. "Don't worry. We'll get you all dolled up. Won't we, girls?"

Jade groaned inwardly. That's what she was afraid of. How could she tell her mom and sisters that she didn't feel comfortable wearing the outfits they favored? Yes, they looked glamorous, but she felt like a fake. Like a child playing dress up. She thought briefly of wearing the dress from the Ranchers' Reception, but her mom had already given it a thumbs-down. Not because she didn't look good in it but because she'd already worn it to the summer gala, and she'd attempted to wear it for her date with Heath.

So here she was planning out the strategy for today's shopping trip.

"Maybe we should let Jade pick out her own dress," Sabrina suggested.

Wendy frowned. "And miss out on all the fun?"

And that's why she was going along with this, Jade thought. She hated to disappoint her one remaining parent. She'd been a disappointment to Casper. Been there. Done that. Didn't want to do it with her mom too.

"Do you have any idea what you'd like to wear to this reunion?" Wendy asked.

"Clothes," Jade said but immediately regretted the snide comment. Her mother didn't deserve that, but it was situations like this that made her feel so inadequate. Her mother and her sisters all had an innate fashion sense, and she didn't. She was a jeans-and-T-shirt kind of gal. The only thing she wore that could be describe as fashionable were her colorful and sometimes decorated Chuck Taylors. Like the ones she had on now that she'd ordered off Etsy. They were hunter green and embroidered with fanciful mushrooms. But she figured calling her Chucks a fashion statement was stretching the truth a bit.

"Very funny. Don't worry, we'll help you pick out something fabulous. We plan to make a day of it."

Jade wanted to tell her mother that she was thirty-three years old and could pick out her own clothes. But she knew Wendy and her sisters thought they were being helpful. She hated feeling this way, but shopping with the women in her family only served to show how different Jade was from them.

She remembered Casper telling Wendy to "do something with that girl" and her mom sticking up for her, telling her father that there was nothing wrong with their daughter just because she didn't like to wear frilly dresses or, when she did, she managed to get dirty.

Still doing that, Dad, she silently admitted, remembering the evening of her ill-fated first date with Heath.

She wished she'd been able to connect with her dad before his death, set things right between them, but she hadn't and now it was too late. A regret she'd have to live with. She wasn't about to let anything like that happen with her mother.

Plastering on a smile, she managed, "I'm looking forward to shopping and makeovers."

"Heath won't know what hit him," Wendy said with a triumphant gleam.

Jade suppressed a groan. Her mom was talking like this reunion was an actual party, but Jade saw it as an ordeal to survive. Or was there more to this? Was Wendy hoping to get Jade happily settled in a relationship like her two sisters? She didn't want to think about it. Too afraid of being disappointed.

She needed to keep in mind that her relationship with Heath wasn't real, it was based on a lie fabricated to save face in front of high school bullies. Sure, when he was kissing her, it felt real, as real as his lips on hers. But she knew in her heart that this time with Heath was only temporary.

"Should we go to Houston or Dallas?" Wendy asked after the waitress dropped off their breakfasts.

Jade frowned. "Oh, I doubt if we need to go that far."

"Well, our choices in and around Chatelaine are pretty limited," her mom reminded her. "It's not like we're going to find you a dress and shoes at GreatStore."

Jade started to say, *Why not?* but clamped her mouth shut before the words slipped out. Why make this any harder than it already was by being petty?

"And you'll come to the Castle for a spa treatment before the reunion."

"That's where Alexis and Nina had been." The two who'd started this whole thing. But a voice reminded Jade that this was her own fault. She's the one who opened her mouth.

Wendy nodded. "Yes, we sent invitations out."

"And you picked Nina because she's such an important influencer?" Jade asked.

"I'm sure that was the reason, but I didn't do the picking. I hired a publicist to take care of that. Jade, I apologize for that. If I had known how she'd treated you, I wouldn't have invited her."

Jade shrugged. "She's an influencer and can send a lot of business your way. I understand why she was invited. I only wish I hadn't run into her and Alexis. I wouldn't be in all this trouble now."

"Trouble? I would hardly call it that. You've met a wonderful man and are spending time with him. How could that be a bad thing?"

Because I'm spending time with a wonderful man, that's why.

If she wasn't careful, she'd start believing in the lie herself. And that was asking for trouble.

Heath spotted Jade sitting with her mother and sisters as soon as he walked into the diner. He still wasn't sure if he should be doing this. Maybe she didn't want to be rescued. What gave him the right to interfere?

He might be out of line, but after listening to Jade last night and hearing the apprehension in her voice over this proposed shopping trip, he couldn't just sit back and do nothing. Besides, if she preferred going with her mother and sisters, she could simply say no to his suggestion.

He glanced across the crowded restaurant at Jade before striding toward them. The look on Jade's face had him going forward. Couldn't her mother and sisters see how miserable she was? She might not thank him for what he was about to do, but he had to chance it.

"Ladies, hello," he said as he approached the table. "I'm so glad I ran into you."

Dahlia gave him a speculative glance. "It's good to see you too, Heath."

Did Jade's sister suspect why he was here? "I hate to intrude on this family moment, but could I borrow Jade for a minute?"

Dahlia smiled at him. "Of course. We don't mind at all. Do we, Mom?"

Heath returned Dahlia's smile, but he was also smiling because he had a feeling she knew what he was doing. She obviously approved. At least he had one ally.

Jade got up and followed him to an empty table, but they didn't sit. "What's going on? Is something wrong? Did—"

Heath cut off her questions with a kiss. He knew Wendy and the others could see him with Jade. Hell, everyone in the place saw that. After he pulled away from Jade's delectable mouth, he glanced over and saw

Wendy's grin. Okay, maybe he wouldn't be causing a family rift by doing this.

"Nothing's wrong," he reassured her. "I have to make a quick trip to Houston to personally approve some changes to our drone project."

"Oh, so I won't see you tonight?" Her tone held disappointment.

"That's just it. I'm hoping you'll go with me."

"Oh." Her eyes widened and her gaze locked onto his. Moistening her lips, she said, "My mom and sisters want to take me shopping for an outfit for the reunion today."

"The meeting won't take me long and we could go to Nordstrom to shop and then to supper."

"Nordstrom?" she asked with a twinkle in her eyes.

He grinned. "Yeah, I've heard you can't even trust a town that doesn't have one."

She laughed and glanced back to where her mother and sisters sat.

Now that he'd asked her, he found that he hoped she'd say yes. "I still owe you a dinner. Remember? Not that I didn't enjoy Wendy's lasagna."

She shook her head. "That was my fault."

"Charlie's fault."

"But he's my dog, so ultimately my fault."

He raised his eyebrows. "So you'll come?"

"Hmm. That would mean I'd have to bail out on the shopping trip with my mom and sisters." She chewed on her bottom lip and glanced over at their booth. "But okay. Why not? I can make it up to them by agreeing to the spa day they want to do."

"You're sure? I don't want to cause any trouble." And he meant it. He reached for her hand.

"It's fine. Really," she said and squeezed his hand as they made their way back to the table.

"Heath needs to take a trip to Houston today and wants me to go with him."

"Why does he need you?" Wendy's brow furrowed.

"Maybe he likes her company," Dahlia whispered and threw her mother a look.

Heath silently thanked Dahlia. "I'm sorry to spoil your fun shopping trip today, but I'd really love Jade's company during the drive, and I wanted to show her the new drone prototypes."

"You do?" Wendy asked.

"Why is that so hard to believe?" Dahlia winked at her sister. "Jade is great company."

"Of course she is," Wendy agreed. "I meant why did he want her to see his prototype?"

Sabrina giggled and Wendy poked her. "I was talking about the drones. That *is* what we're talking about, isn't it?"

"Yes, my company is hoping to use them for help farmers eradicate weeds without spraying fields full of pesticides. I've already started giving a series of talks for the students at Jade's day camps. If she sees what I'm talking about it will be more helpful to plan things."

"That makes sense," Sabrina and Dahlia said at the same time.

Wendy nodded. "Yes, I suppose it does." She glanced at her oldest daughter. "Go ahead, honey. We can reschedule our shopping trip."

After they'd left the restaurant, Heath said, "I hope I haven't gotten you into hot water with your family over this."

"You might be the one in hot water. They'll start thinking you're serious about all this."

"Who says I'm not?"

Jade blushed. "Well... I..."

Heath decided to let her off the hook by changing the subject. Or was he letting *himself* off the hook? "Last night when we talked, I got the impression you were uncomfortable with their shopping plans."

She blew out her breath noisily through her lips. "I always feel so inadequate when it comes to picking out fancy clothes. They mean well but..."

"That's because you're not being true to who you are. Yes, your mother and sisters are stylish, but so are you."

"Yeah, right." She rolled her eyes.

"It's true." He reached for her hand again and squeezed gently. "If you chose things that were true to who you are, you'd feel more comfortable. Trying to imitate someone else never works."

"You sound like you've had experience." She gave him a look.

They reached his car, and he opened the passenger door for her. "Not with clothes but with my company. I found a niche market with smaller farmers and ranchers rather than the big corporate ones. That's when I was the most successful."

"So, you're more dedicated to helping than getting rich?" She settled in the seat and reached for the seat belt.

"I've been lucky that the money followed, and now I

can use some of it for research and development to help smaller family farms and ranches. I'm glad my technology helps large industrial farms and ranches, but I don't want it to stop there. I know right now not all the high tech is affordable for the smaller family farms and ranches, but that's why I'm working on improvements. If I can streamline the process, I can help even the smallest family farm. At the moment, I'm setting up cooperatives so they can share the equipment."

"You mean like renting it out on an as-needed basis?" she asked.

"Exactly. I've created a foundation for the initial layout of funds but after that, I'm hoping the rental fees can support it."

He shut the passenger door and went around the hood of the SUV and slid into the passenger seat.

"Why are you looking at me like that?" he asked when she continued to stare at him. He glanced in the rearview mirror. "Do I have something in my teeth?"

"No. I just thought that when you first came to town that you were like Casper."

"You thought I was like your *father*?" He wasn't sure how to feel about this.

"Yes."

"It's good that I'm not?" At least he hoped that's what she meant.

"Very good. He only cared about the money and chasing what he considered success."

Heath started the engine and eased out of the parking spot and onto the main road. He wanted money and success as much as the next person, but it wasn't his main goal.

Having met his sisters he considered family one of the most important aspects of life. Of course he needed to uncover the truth about the circumstances surrounding his birth before starting one of his own.

As Jade listened to Heath, one thing became clear. She wasn't just falling in love...she had a feeling she'd already taken that tumble.

Now that she'd gotten to know Heath Blackwood, she didn't have to be upset with herself for having a crush on someone who might be like her dad. Someone who chased success to the exclusion of everything else and who wouldn't look twice at her because she didn't fit the profile of the sort of woman a rich man wants on his arm. She could just imagine what her father would have said about her running a petting zoo and camps for underprivileged children.

On the drive to Houston, they talked about food, movies and whatever else came to mind in a meandering and comfortable conversation.

Seeing a traveling carnival set up in an open field on the side of the road made Jade sigh. She'd always loved them but rarely had the opportunity to go because Casper had always said Windhams didn't participate in such low-brow activities. Well, she had and did it every chance she got even if it meant sneaking out to attend.

A thought occurred to her, and she sat up straighter.

"What is it?" he asked.

"I'm not a Windham anymore," she blurted.

"I know. You all changed your last name to Fortune, but it's my understanding that happened a while ago."

"It did."

He glanced at her for a second then turned back to concentrate on the road ahead,

She sighed. What the heck? She may as well explain. So what if he thought she was weird? "I saw that Ferris wheel over there."

He looked over to the field and nodded. "Looks like one of those traveling carnivals. But what does that have to do with being a Fortune or a Windham?"

She explained how her dad had felt about such activities.

He nodded. "So, since you're not a Windham you can attend all the tacky carnivals you want."

"You think they're tacky?" Disappointment lanced through her.

"Sorry. Poor choice of words. I have never been to one, so I shouldn't pass judgment."

"No, you shouldn't," she said with a little huff.

"I honestly didn't mean to offend you." He reached for her hand.

She seized on something he'd said. "You've never been to one? Ever?"

"Never."

"That's…that's terrible. A giant gaping hole in your life."

He laughed. "I never realized I was so deprived."

"Well, you are. We really should rectify that."

"We should, but I wasn't lying about my meeting."

She heaved a sigh. "And I need to find a dress for the reunion."

"But neither one will take all day," he said. He spared another glance at her. "Or will it?"

"I am not a big shopper. Believe me, I don't plan on dragging you from store to store all day. That was my mother's plan, not mine. Besides, I can always take a rain check with her and my sisters for a day of shopping."

"You make it sound like a fate worse than death."

She stared down at her hands in her lap. "They mean well."

"I'm sure the Ferris wheel will still be there on the way back."

Her eyes lit up. "You mean it? We can stop?"

"I don't see why not," he said.

Today was turning out a lot better than Jade had thought when she got up in morning. But she was finding that any day that included time spent with Heath was a good day.

Their relationship might not last beyond the reunion, but she decided that she was going to jump into every moment as if it were the last—since it very well might be—and enjoy herself.

Heath was glad he had given into temptation and invited Jade to accompany him to his meeting with the research and development folks in Houston. She had offered to wait somewhere else while he conducted business, but he wanted to show her his latest prototype. *Show off is more like it*, a voice taunted, but he brushed it aside. So what if it was true?

After showing her the prototype drones, they indeed went to Nordstrom, where she found an understated blue dress that went perfect with the sapphire ring he'd given her. True to her word, she didn't take long to pick out an outfit, including shoes. He bought a new shirt to go with one of his business suits.

"Where would you like to stop for supper?" he asked as he stowed their purchases in the G Wagon. "I didn't make a reservation because I wasn't sure what time we'd be done or where in the city we might end up."

"Well…" She dragged out the word as she chewed on her lower lip. "I'll bet that carnival has corn dogs and funnel cakes."

"You're joking, right? You actually mean you'd prefer deep-fried dogs and pastry to a nice dinner with candle-light at some fancy restaurant?" He honestly didn't mind either way, but he enjoyed teasing her. Lately, when he thought about Jade, he was thinking of more long term than the reunion. He couldn't be sure if she felt the same way, but if he was reading some of the signals right, and lord knew he might be all wrong, this wasn't one-sided.

"What's wrong with corn dogs and funnel cakes? Or cotton candy and candy apples? Ooh, I bet they have those too."

Her enthusiastic comments brought his thoughts out of his head, and he started the engine. "Who knew you were such a junk food junkie?"

"It's not *junk food*, and I'm a connoisseur of carni-val food."

He raised an eyebrow and spared her a quick glance

as he pulled out of the shopping center's parking lot. "A connoisseur?"

"And don't you forget it." She laughed.

"Duly noted," he assured her.

"So, you really don't mind stopping at the carnival?"

He heard the wistful note in her voice and said, "I don't mind, and since I'll be with a connoisseur, I'm sure she'll steer me to the right booths for amazing food."

"That's the spirit," she said, giggling like a schoolgirl.

As they had done on the way to the city that morning, they chatted easily as he drove through late afternoon traffic and left the city behind.

"It's actually a county fair," he remarked as he pulled into the grassy field doubling as a parking lot.

Without even waiting for him to come around to her side, she hopped out of the Mercedes once he'd parked. "I can't tell you how much I appreciate this," she said as they crossed the field toward the entrance booth.

He took her hand in his and only dropped it to get out his wallet so he could buy entry tickets and tickets for food, rides and games on the midway.

Sticking the tickets in his pocket, he reached for her hand again. They passed several large canvas tents on their way to the Ferris wheel, which Jade had insisted on riding first.

"It's my favorite," she told him.

"What's the matter?" she asked when he dragged his feet. "You're not afraid of heights, are you?"

"Me? Afraid? No way. It's just that these rides are put up and taken down so many times, there's no telling what sort of wear and tear they're subjected to."

"But that's just it. These people know what they're doing. They're professionals."

He raised an eyebrow and gave her a skeptical look.

She grinned at him. "Look, if you want to stay down here, you can. I won't think any less of you."

"If you go, I go," he said with as much of a glower as he could muster. Despite any misgivings over the integrity of the rides, he was having fun, and he had Jade's enthusiasm to thank for that.

They boarded the Ferris wheel. He wasn't afraid of heights as such; he just liked having his two feet on the ground better. But he meant it; he was going where Jade was.

When their car got to the top, it stopped.

Of course it stopped, he thought ruefully.

"You're supposed to kiss me," Jade told him. "That's the rule if you get stopped at the top."

"It is?"

She gave a firm nod of her head. "Well, if it isn't, it should be."

So he obliged and kissed her. His lips on hers made him forget he was sitting on a rickety Ferris wheel high in the sky. All that mattered to him was her soft, sweet lips pressed against his.

She gasped and pulled away when the Ferris wheel started to move with a jerk and a rocking motion. Then she laughed with glee and he found himself laughing too.

Apparently, he found a cure for his dislike of heights, and she was sitting right beside him.

After the ride they wandered among the crowd of fair-goers. The smell of grilling meat and deep-fried food permeated the air around them. Not exactly the candlelight and wine he'd envisioned for tonight with Jade, but one look at the excitement and contentment on her face told him this was the right choice. And he had to admit that he was enjoying the evening too. The music from the rides and the buzz of excitement from the fairgoers filled the air and provided a frenetic backdrop to their evening. Jade seemed to thrive on it.

Instead of corn dogs, they stopped at food cart that sold Greek gyro sandwiches. They found a spot at a picnic table and ate their supper. After they'd finished their sandwiches and tossed the trash into a bin, she pointed to a cart advertising funnel cakes, her eyes aglow with enthusiasm. "Look. Dessert."

They enjoyed the funnel cakes while standing to the side of the cart.

"So, what else haven't you had a chance to do at a carnival?" he asked as she munched on her funnel cake.

"You haven't won me a stuffed animal yet."

He groaned. "You do know those games are rigged. And not in the player's favor."

She grinned and hooked her arm through his. "I have every bit of faith in you."

"Wait." Heath reached out and stopped her before she began walking again.

"What?"

He reached over and brushed her cheek with his fingertips. "You had some powdered sugar on you."

"That's the only trouble with funnel cakes."

He wouldn't exactly call it trouble since it gave him an excuse to touch her.

They enjoyed the next several hours at the carnival. Heath managed to win her a small stuffed animal. To his embarrassment, it was one of the tiniest prizes offered. But Jade didn't seem to care. She acted as if it were the most coveted treasure.

"I'll do better next time," he promised.

"I'm perfectly content with this one," she assured him.

And he was perfectly content with the way they'd spent their evening.

Chapter Ten

Jade checked herself in the full-length mirror in the master bath. She had to admit that the woman staring back at her looked fabulous, if she did say so herself. Thanks to her mom, she'd spent a greater part of the day at the spa at Fortune's Castle. Evidently she'd received some of the same treatment that Alexis and Nina had enjoyed.

Jade picked up the blue satin clutch purse she'd purchased on the trip to Houston and glanced at herself one last time. Yes, she looked good, but it wasn't her staring back from the mirror. It was a fairy-tale version of Jade Fortune.

But life wasn't like a fairy tale.

"Except for tonight," she told her reflection.

Tonight was *her* fairy tale, and she was going to enjoy it and not worry about tomorrow.

Right on time, a knock sounded at the door, and she went to answer it.

She opened it and stood speechless. Dressed in an impeccably tailored dark blue suit with a pristine white shirt open at the neck, Heath took her breath away.

He frowned and touched the open neck of his shirt. "Should I have worn a tie?"

"What?" She continued to stare for a second longer. Shaking her head, she whispered, "No. You're fine."

"Good." He stepped inside and his gaze swept the room. "No Charlie tonight?"

"He's with my mom. I wasn't sure what time we'd be back," Jade said and shut the door. "Besides, this way there's less chance of any sort of wardrobe malfunctions."

He laughed. "I suppose that's true, but I kinda miss the guy."

"So do I, but believe me, he's getting spoiled by my mom."

Heath stood staring at her, the silence stretching until she finally cleared her throat. "Something wrong?"

She'd been convinced she looked great, but maybe Heath didn't agree. But he'd already seen the dress, so it couldn't be that. She glanced down at herself in case she'd managed to—

"Hey, hey," he said and used his hand to lift her chin and stare into her eyes. "Nothing's wrong."

She swallowed. "Then why are you staring at me?"

"Because you are beautiful." A slow smile spread across his handsome face. "Perfection."

She laughed but was secretly thrilled. "Well, it's obvious that you need those glasses for more than reading. But you do make me feel beautiful. And more than that, you make me feel special."

"That's because you *are* special."

Her chin still captured by his hand, he leaned over and brought his lips in a sweet, reverent kiss.

The tenderness in his touch made her breath catch in her throat.

Lifting his head, he said, "We'd better get going or we'll be late."

Heath pulled the SUV into the parking lot at the country club where the reunion was being held. The large white building was lit up both inside and out. Three steps led to a small landing where double doors were thrown open, inviting people inside.

He stopped at the valet parking stand. "Pretty swanky for a high school reunion."

"Well, it was a swanky high school," she said.

"It didn't change the high school experience though, did it?" he asked. He'd always thought that his circumstances, having a single mother who struggled to provide for her son and being a bit of a social misfit, had been the cause of his experiences. But Jade had helped him to see that wasn't the only reason. Jade had been part of a prominent family, and as beautiful as she was now, he had to believe she'd been attractive in high school. Since meeting Jade, he had to admit she'd changed a lot of his ways of thinking about things.

"Not at all," she was saying.

The valet opened her door, and she stepped out of the SUV. Heath got out and handed the keys to the attendant. Going around the front of the vehicle, Heath met up with Jade and took her arm. "Ready?"

"Again, I want to thank you for this."

He shook his head. "No thanks necessary. This is my pleasure."

And he meant it. Attending a high school reunion might not be at the top of his list of things he wanted to do on a Saturday night, but being with Jade made him happy. It didn't matter where he was, as long as he was with her. The fact he was helping her in front of those snotty former classmates was a plus. The things they'd said to Jade that day still rankled him.

"Did I tell you how gorgeous you look tonight?" he asked as they climbed the steps to the entrance.

"Only about a dozen times."

"Then let's make it a baker's dozen."

Once inside, Jade checked them in at the table set up and manned by a former classmate that she only vaguely remembered.

But it appeared the woman remembered her. "Good to see you, Jade. I was wondering what you'd gotten up to since graduation. Nina and Alexis say you're running some sort of animal thing in Chatelaine?"

"It's a petting zoo," Jade told her as she pulled the backing off her name tag to expose the sticky side.

"She's way too modest," Heath said. He suspected this person wasn't going to treat Jade any better than those other two. He put an arm around Jade's waist. "She also runs day camps and workshops for kids to teach them about how technology is the future for ranching and farming, both important industries for this state."

The woman eyed him closely. "And you must be Mr. Fortune?"

Heath smiled at the woman. "No, it's Blackwood. Heath Blackwood."

He couldn't help grinning, thinking about the Bond

movies. Maybe he should have tried out a Sean Connery accent. And totally embarrassed himself.

The woman's mouth dropped open. "You're the Heath Blackwood of Blackwood AgriTech?"

"That's him all right," Jade said proudly.

"Well, we're honored to have you here, Mr. Blackwood."

"And I'm honored to be here…with Jade," he said before they moved on.

They'd barely entered the packed ballroom when Nina and Alexis spotted them.

"Jade Windham… I mean Fortune. You came and you even brought your, uh, fiancé with you," Alexis said when she saw Jade and Heath.

"I hate to let her out of my sight," Heath murmured, putting his arm around Jade.

"I can see why. If she were with me, I'd want everyone to know she was off the market." A short, stocky man wearing wire-rimmed glasses and a bow tie glided up. He grinned. "Is that you Jade Windham? Remember me? Roger Stackhouse. I was president of the Computer Science Club."

Nina and Alexis snorted, but Roger ignored them. He obviously knew them well.

Jade smiled and shook Roger's hand. "Actually, it's Jade Fortune now."

Roger chuckled. "As if being a Windham wasn't enough. Now, you're a Fortune. How did that come about?"

"It's on my mother's side. She found out she was the long-lost granddaughter of Wendell Fortune. My mother changed her name to honor the connection, and we followed suit."

"All of you?" Roger asked.

"All six of us, but with my sisters getting engaged and marrying, they didn't really keep the Fortune names for very long. But my brothers will presumably have it for the rest of their lives."

Roger nodded, then a look of surprised recognition came over his face. "And you're Heath Blackwood of Blackwood AgriTech!"

Heath nodded.

"Well, it's certainly a pleasure to meet you." Roger beamed.

Jade stood next to Heath and listened to him and Roger talking about computer technology. She noticed Nina and Alexis roll their eyes and wander off like predators deprived of prey.

"It's been great chatting with you, Roger, but I promised Jade we'd dance," Heath said.

"Oh yeah. Sure, sure. It was good seeing you again, Jade."

The band was playing a slow one and Heath took her in his arms. In his strong embrace, Jade forgot everything else. Even seeing Alexis and Nina again meant nothing.

"I'm sorry for that woman calling you Mr. Fortune. Talk about awkward," she said as Heath glided her around the dance floor.

"It's okay. I actually don't mind not being recognized. It can get old fast."

She gazed up at him and nodded. "I'll bet."

"It's true. You never know if someone wants to talk to you because they think you're interesting or they're just interested in what you can do for them."

Now she regretted her remark. "I guess I hadn't thought about it that way."

"First being a Windham then a Fortune, you must have run into that," he mused.

"Not really. I guess people didn't expect to run into Casper Windham's daughter waiting tables or selling lingerie at Nordstrom. When they'd ask if I was any relation, I usually said no." She didn't want it getting back to Casper, but more importantly, she didn't want to explain why she wasn't successful like her siblings.

"Earning an honest living is nothing to be ashamed of," Heath told her.

"No, but if Casper found out that someone saw his daughter waitressing, he would have gone ballistic. Said I was ruining the family name."

"Well, I never had a family name to ruin," he said.

"I think Blackwood is a very fine name and one you should take pride in. You're a self-made man and have a lot to be proud of."

A jolt of awareness shot through her when her gaze met his. Judging from the slight darkening of his eyes, he felt it too.

"Thanks."

They danced before and after the lavish meal.

"I have to confess I didn't think I was going to enjoy this, but I am," Jade said as the evening was winding down and people started leaving. Having people envious of her was a whole new experience.

Deep down, she'd been dreading the reunion, but now she was sorry to see it end. Being with Heath and dancing with him was like a dream come true. She felt like a true Cinderella, but like the fairy tale, it was time to leave the ball.

"So I was thinking," Heath began as they waited for the valet to bring the car around, "would you be interested in staying in Cactus Grove tonight?" He held up his hands, palms out. "No pressure. If you don't want to, that's fine."

"You mean instead of returning to Chatelaine?"

"Yeah, we could stay in town or go somewhere else where there's more choice of hotels. You did say your mom is watching Charlie."

"That's true. I wasn't sure how late we'd get back, so I said I'd pick him up in the morning. She wouldn't even have to know we didn't return to Chatelaine after the reunion."

He frowned. "You don't want her to know you spent the night with me?"

"Oh, no, it's not that. I was just saving you her efforts at matchmaking. Since my two sisters are in relationships, she's trying to get me into one too."

"I think I can handle the pressure."

Did this mean he was as interested in her as she was with him? Sounded like maybe he was wanting to take this to the next level. Question was, did *she*? "I didn't bring a change of clothes or any toiletries with me."

He shrugged, his face blank. "The hotel will supply

any toiletries you might need. We can shop for clothes for you tomorrow."

Somewhere inside, a voice whispered words of caution. She hadn't known Heath for very long. Should she be doing this?

Any other time or with any other man, she might have heeded the warning voice, but when she was with Heath, nothing mattered except the two of them.

"I'd love to stay here tonight."

They found a hotel within the town limits. As Heath checked them in, he glanced at her, a question in his blue eyes. She smiled and nodded to indicate that she was still on board with spending the night together.

After getting the room keys, he took her hand and led her to the elevator. Once inside, the air seemed to crackle between them.

This was really happening, she thought as they exited the elevator and walked down the corridor. When he inserted the key, they all but tumbled into the room.

He used his foot to shut the door behind them and pulled her into his arms. Their mouths crashed together as he led them over to the king-sized bed.

They toppled onto the bed without losing contact.

All urgency gone, he kissed her slowly, thoroughly, leaving her trembling beneath him. His mouth touched and tasted, overwhelming her until she melted. Jade didn't want the kiss to ever end. She wanted to drown in it. She wanted to lose herself completely.

He kissed, stroked and explored her body making her feel not just feminine but desired and special. When he had worked her into another frenzy, he ripped open the foil packet. Nudging her entrance, he moved slowly as her body adjusted to him. Another gesture that made her feel treasured. He set a rhythm that had her climbing toward another release. Was that even possible? He put his hand between their bodies and found that sensitive bud. Not just possible...*inevitable*.

"Yes, please." She writhed and twisted on the mattress; the sheets clutched in her fists.

One last powerful thrust, and they simultaneously fell over the edge.

They lay entwined as their breathing slowed, his fingers making lazy trails across her bare skin.

"You're very talented," she whispered.

His gaze riveted on hers, he brought his hand to her face and used his fingertips to trace the sprinkling of freckles across the bridge of her nose and the top of her cheeks. The warmth from his fingers lingered on her skin, raising the hair on the back of her neck.

His mouth captured hers again and she was lost in the tantalizing sensation that was Heath.

Jade awoke to an empty bed the next morning. She glanced around the room, but Heath wasn't there, and the door to the bathroom was open, so he wasn't inside there either.

Maybe he was out getting coffee or breakfast, she thought as she scrambled around on the floor to pick up her discarded clothing.

As much as she loved last night's dress, she wrinkled her nose at having to put it back on this morning.

Before she made it to the bathroom, the hotel door opened, and Heath walked in with several shopping bags.

"You're awake," he said as he came to her and gave her a kiss. "You were sleeping so soundly, I hated to wake you before I left. I was hoping I'd get back before you woke up."

"I've only been awake for a few minutes."

"Perfect timing." He handed her a bag.

"What's this?" She peeked inside.

"For today. As much as I love that dress, I figured you would prefer being more comfortable for the return home."

She pulled out a pair of jeans, a comfy looking sweatshirt and some underwear. There was even a pair of Converse high-tops in the bag.

"I can't guarantee everything will fit, but I checked your sizes from what you'd been wearing last night."

She threw her arms around him and hugged him. "That's so thoughtful of you."

After showering together, they dressed and went downstairs for a leisurely breakfast before getting back on the road to Chatelaine.

Chapter Eleven

Several days after their weekend together in Cactus Grove, Heath asked Jade to accompany him to visit Billy, the boy he'd spoken to during his workshop.

"Is something wrong?" she asked.

"No. I have something for him."

"Okay, he should be home from school by now."

He saw her inquisitive gaze, but he didn't tell her what he'd done. As it was, he was crossing his fingers that the boy would like his gift. He'd never done anything like this before.

Heath parked the G Wagon in front of a small craftsman-style home in a solid working-class neighborhood of Chatelaine.

They went to the door, and it opened before they could knock. The boy must have seen them through the window. Jade had called ahead and spoke with Billy's mother to be sure they were home.

"You came to see me!" Billy greeted them.

"We sure did." Heath greeted Billy's mother and handed the gift bag to the boy.

Billy pulled a book out of the bag. "What's this?"

"I believe people call it a memory book. Your mom

and some people in town gave me pictures and told stories about your dad."

Billy's eyes widened and he clutched the book to his chest. "You mean this book is all about my dad?"

"It sure is. There's even some stuff in there about when he was your age."

"Really?"

"Yes, really."

"And I can keep it? For my very own?" the boy whispered.

"Absolutely," Heath assured him.

"I can't thank you enough for this," his mother told Heath. "Please sit down. Can I get you some coffee? I made a pot."

Billy sat and looked at his book, carefully turning the pages.

They stayed for coffee and some homemade cookies.

Once they were back outside and heading to the Mercedes, Jade turned to him.

"That was so thoughtful of you," Jade told him, her eyes welling with tears.

He shrugged but was grateful for her words. "I only thought of it. Others did the work of gathering the information and putting it all together for the book. They deserve the credit."

"They wouldn't have done it if you hadn't come up with the idea and asked them to do it."

"The kid was worried about preserving memories of his dad. I didn't want him messing up his life because he was worried over something I could easily help fix." He swallowed hard. "Not that I or anybody else could help fix the fact he'd lost his dad. If I could ease his pain some, it's worth it."

"Because you know what it's like not to remember your dad," she murmured.

"I'm familiar with some of what he might be going through not having a father."

Jade stood on her toes and kissed his cheek. "You're a special man, Heath Blackwood."

"What good is all this success if I can't help ease a young boy's concerns?"

"And that's why I love you," she said.

At Jade's words, Heath's hands gripped the steering wheel tighter. He mumbled something, but he couldn't bring himself to say the words back at her.

Back at Jade's log home, he went inside and kissed her as soon as they were inside. After greeting Charlie, Heath carried Jade to the bedroom.

He needed this, needed to be close to her one more time. This was coming to an end. It had to, because he was no closer to finding out the truth surrounding his birth.

But he couldn't let her go. Not yet.

Jade told herself this was his way of saying he loved her. He might have trouble with the words, but he'd shown her with his actions. He loved her as thoroughly as he had the night of the reunion. Once again, she told him she loved him.

Afterward, she snuggled up to him, but something was off. His body might be right next to her in the bed, but she suspected his mind was elsewhere, closed off.

She wanted to take the coward's way out and ignore that Heath had no response to her declaration. She probably shouldn't have said the words so soon, but she couldn't hold it in any longer.

If she didn't ask him about it, he might not tell her, and she could bury her head in the sand, pretend she hadn't said anything. Or claim that it was just one of those things people said and that she didn't mean it in the literal sense. That might buy her some time before he told her they were through and the fairy tale she'd been living would be over.

But she couldn't do that, because she *had* meant it. She was worth more than silence. The ironic part of the whole situation was that being with Heath is what taught her she was worth more than accepting a less than ideal situation.

In hindsight, she knew that if the situation at the Daily Grind with Nina and Alexis had happened today, Jade would probably have handled the whole thing differently. Instead of feeling like she'd been put on the spot, she hoped she would be able to put those two in their place without resorting to lying or pretending she was something she wasn't.

She was proud of the classes and day camps she offered. As Heath pointed out, she was helping shape future ranchers and farmers, and maybe one of her students would end up helping to revolutionize agricultural tech like Heath was doing.

Might as well get this over with, she thought. "So are you going to tell me what's wrong?"

"What's makes you think something's wrong?" He pulled away.

"Because of what just happened."

"What just happened was that we made love. So, why would you think something's off?" he asked, but he had guilt stamped all over his features.

"We didn't make love. We had sex. You went through the motions."

A muscle ticked in his jaw. "Are you complaining?"

"What? No. It's always great with you."

"Then what is it?"

"It's just…it felt as though you were pulling back emotionally."

He opened his mouth, and she held up her hand to stop him. "Let me finish before I lose my nerve. It was as if you were putting walls up, protecting yourself."

"Do you want the truth?" he asked, a muscle ticked in his jaw.

No! I want to stay in this sensual bubble a little longer. "Always…even if it hurts."

His expression darkened. "I'm trying to protect you, Jade."

"Protect me from what?" she asked, fear and anger knotting inside her.

"From me."

Frustration clawed at the back of her throat. "Why would I need protecting from you?"

"Because I know you want a home and family." He ran a hand through his hair.

"And?"

"And… I can't give that to you." He blew out a ragged breath.

"And you know this how, why?" Ice slowly spread through her stomach.

"Because I can't get involved with anyone until I find out the truth about who I am."

"What are you saying?" she asked, searching for a plausible explanation. "You're Heath Blackwood. Entrepreneur, a man who loved his mother, a man who cares about farmers and ranchers. A man who wants to help even the small family farmers with his advances in technology."

He shook his head, and she reached out and touched him, squeezed his arm. "It doesn't matter who or what you came from. All that matters is who you are now."

"That's easy for you to say. You know who your father is and the circumstances of your birth."

"I do, but that doesn't—"

"Yes, it does!" He jerked away from her touch. "You wouldn't understand."

Jade flinched at the anger in his voice, but she refused to back down. If this was going to end, she would know she at least tried. She'd know she fought for what they had, what they'd meant to one another. She couldn't give up without a fight. Heath meant too much to her.

"Try me," she said, her voice full of challenge.

"I don't know why my father never acknowledged me. My mother would never tell me, and she got upset every time I tried to push for answers so I eventually gave up."

"And that's okay. Maybe you aren't meant to know."

"I have to know, damn it. Why are you so accepting of this unknown?"

"Because I love you, damn it!" As far as declarations of love went, this had to be the worst one so far. What was wrong with her?

His jaw hardened and he glared down at her. "No. You can't. I won't let you."

"You won't *let* me? If that don't beat all, I swear."

"This whole relationship wasn't supposed to be real."

"Yeah, well, I broke the ground rules," she admitted thickly. "It's not like I planned it or anything."

"Thank goodness for small favors."

"That's cruel and beneath you, Heath."

Regret washed over his features and his tone softened. "You're right. I'm sorry. And I'm sorry that you were expecting something more from me. I was quite clear from the beginning that I wasn't looking for long term."

"That's true so there's no need to apologize. That's all on me. My brain heard what you said, but my heart refused to listen."

"You should have listened," he told her wearily.

"Duh. I know that now. Maybe you need to leave." *Because I want to sob and cry.* But she didn't say that out loud, but she did say, "And please take this with you."

She removed the ring and held it out to him.

He shook his head. "I don't—"

"Please."

Reluctantly, he held out his hand and she dropped the ring into it.

She got out of bed and padded barefoot into the adjoining bathroom and shut the door. She threw the lock with a quiet click.

Heath was gone when she finally emerged.

Jade pulled into her driveway and parked. It had been three days since her breakup with Heath. Three days of yawning emptiness, of longing. She squeezed her eyes shut as she struggled to quell the dragging sense of loss threatening to engulf her.

In the beginning she'd tried to protect herself but her feelings for Heath had eventually made that impossible. She was sure he'd developed feelings for her too and that was the sharpest knife of all.

Sighing, she exited her pickup. Life went on, right? She'd stopped at the mailbox station at the end of the road leading to all the properties on the ranch. The envelope looked like a card or invitation.

She opened the envelope and pulled out an invitation. To a wedding. *A mystery wedding.* The whole town had been buzzing about it. It was an invitation, along with a note requesting she bring a photo of herself as a wedding gift. Why would the happy couple wanted a picture of her? That was strange. She didn't even know who was getting married.

The note also requested that the picture be as close a representation of herself as possible. It might be a bizarre request, but it was certainly easy enough to do.

She got out of the truck and went to her front door. Inserting the key into the lock, she heard dog toenails on the hardwood by the door. Charlie was waiting for her. He would probably be angry with her for not bringing him into town with her.

She opened the door, and the dog greeted her. She gave him a hug and an apology for leaving him behind.

After feeding Charlie, Jade brought the box of photos she kept in the bedroom closet into the living room and set it on the coffee table. She slipped her sneakers off and sat on the couch, drawing her feet up under her. Taking a fortifying sip of wine, she pulled the lid off the box.

It was stuffed with photos. Most were old. People these days keep their photo collections on their phones or their computers. But the invitation stipulated one physical copy that Jade felt most represented herself. Huh. Very odd.

She had picked out one of the photos taken of her when she first moved to the ranch and took over the running of the petting zoo. Sitting back on the couch with Charlie napping beside her, she glanced over at the fireplace.

On the mantel was a picture taken of her the night of the reunion along with one of both her and Heath. She rose and went to the mantel. Her smile was a mile wide in the photo. It was easy to see how happy and excited she was. And why not? She'd been with Heath.

Despite how everything had turned out, she knew that was the picture she needed to use as the gift for the mystery wedding. Things may not have worked out in the end, but that night had been magical. Remembering was bittersweet and she knew that someday those memories would be more sweet than bitter.

Her decision made, she called for Charlie and made her way to her bedroom. Maybe tomorrow would be better. Maybe she'd be closer to those memories bringing a smile along with the tears.

Chapter Twelve

Heath pulled his G Wagon into a spot near the coffee shop. What had gotten into him? Going to see Beau Weatherly wasn't in his nature. As a matter of fact, he'd secretly made fun of the people who did. But after a sleepless night, he was desperate enough to try anything.

Bypassing the takeout window and the seats on the porch that he preferred, Heath went inside and glanced at his watch, Sure enough, Beau was seated at his usual table with his sign that offered Free Life Advice.

He might feel a bit embarrassed by doing this, but he figured the old guy might be the closest he was ever going to get to fatherly advice. He was in luck because no one was waiting to see Beau at the moment.

Heath sat down across from the man.

"Heath," Beau nodded. "Good morning, son."

Heath recalled his earlier thoughts about Beau being a father figure and hoped the warmth in his cheeks hadn't manifested in any sort of blush. Talk about embarrassing.

"So, what can I do for you?" the older man asked.

Heath sighed as if admitting defeat. "I need some advice."

Beau smiled. "That's what I'm here for."

"Yeah, I..." Heath rubbed his jaw. "I'm not sure how much you know about my situation."

"Well, I don't like to pry into your personal affairs, but this *is* Chatelaine, so I probably know as much as you."

Heath chuckled, the act releasing some of the tension that had been building within him. "Small towns. Anyway, I'm debating if I should try visiting Doris Edwards again. I don't know if I should even continue to pursue the truth. I found my sisters and have a...relationship with them."

The word "relationship" wanted to stick in his throat. It reminded him of Jade and what he'd lost. No, not lost. He'd thrown it away. She'd told him she loved him, and he totally disregarded her confession. She'd given him her heart, and he'd handed it back as if it hadn't been the most precious thing in the world.

"Heath? Son, did you have a specific question? I'd like to help, if I can."

Beau's concern touched him. Heath nodded. "I'm wondering if pursuing this thing to find out why my biological father abandoned my mother and myself is the right thing to do. It's been frustrating, to say the least."

It may have cost him the love of his life, but he wasn't about to admit that to Beau. This confessing and seeking advice from the old guy—no matter how wise—had its limits. And Heath had his pride. Thinking back on how happy he'd been when he was with Jade only mocked him now that he'd lost her through his own foolishness.

"Has anything good come of your quest?"

"I found my sisters," Heath replied.

"And that's a good thing?"

"Absolutely. With my mother gone, they're all the family I have left, and I feel blessed to have connected with them."

Steepling his hands, Beau said after a beat, "So, your pursuit of the truth has paid off so far?"

"Yes, sir. I would say it has, but I don't know if continuing to pursue it is the right thing to do."

"Would you be satisfied to know that you stopped trying to uncover the truth?" the man asked. "When you get older and realize the people who are alive today and may have had the answers are gone, will you regret not having pursued it?"

Heath rubbed the back of his neck. The fact he was even asking Beau about this felt like it should be a clue. Trying to deal with Doris Edwards was frustrating, but at least she was here and alive, so he could deal with her. "But what if I learn something I would have preferred not knowing?"

"And what if you learn something you'll be grateful knowing?"

"You've got me there," Heath admitted gruffly.

"Learning the truth won't change who you are or change any of your accomplishments. You'll still be you."

And I'll still have messed things up with Jade.

"You'll be able to go to the woman you love with a clear mind no matter what the outcome is. As I said, son, knowing the truth won't change who you are deep in here," Beau said and tapped his chest.

...go to the woman you love...

Beau's words echoed in Heath's head as he left. Beau was right about that. Was he also right about finding out the truth?

Heath, accompanied by his sister Lily, rounded the corner of Doris Edwards's daughter's modest ranch house. After speaking with Beau, he called his sisters and told them of his plan to see Doris one more time before giving up. Once again, Lily had insisted on coming with him. At first, he wasn't sure if that was such a good idea, but as she'd pointed out, this concerned the triplets too. Plus, on a practical level, she said that having a woman present might help put Doris at ease.

They'd been told the old woman lived in the rear of her daughter's place.

"Ooh, look, it's a tiny house," Lily said.

"It sure is tiny," Heath agreed as they approached what looked to him like a child's fancy playhouse.

"No, no. It's a real honest-to-goodness tiny home." She shook her head when he gave her a puzzled look. "Like all those shows."

"What shows?"

"Oh, I can't remember them all, but they're on the home improvement networks on cable. Shows like *Tiny House Nation* or *Tiny House, Big Living.*"

"Okaaay," he said, dragging the word out.

Lily gave him a playful poke on the shoulder. "It's a thing."

"If you say so," he said and found himself wondering if Jade watched any of those shows. *No, stop thinking about her, or you won't be able to make it through this interview with Doris.* "I prefer a good football game."

"Of course you do." Lily made a noise with her tongue, then she laughed.

Moments later, he knocked on the door of what he now knew was a tiny house.

"You don't have to do this, you know. Whatever happened is in the past," his sister murmured. "We've all found one another now, and that's what's important."

"I want to try at least one more time." At least seeking the truth surrounding his birth gave him something to concentrate on. He didn't want to tell her how miserable he was now that he and Jade had ended things.

No, that wasn't right. Jade hadn't ended anything; he had done all the ending. She had taken a chance and confessed her feelings. He'd been on the edge of that precipice too, but instead of stepping into the scary unknown, he'd faltered. He'd refused to take a chance on love. On happiness. If he had been braver, he'd be with Jade right now. His lack of courage was costing them both.

Just thinking about what he'd given up was like an ice-cold fist twisting his gut. The thought of not seeing Jade again, touching her, kissing her or simply talking with her sent shards of agony shooting through him.

"It's for the best," he muttered under his breath and knocked again on the door. Louder this time.

"What's for the best?" Lily asked, her gaze on Heath.

"What?" He glanced at his sister, realizing he'd almost forgotten she was with him. Most things flew out of his head when he let himself think about Jade. That's why he needed to stop dwelling on her. Put her, and all thoughts of her, in the past where they belonged.

The look Lily gave him said she knew his mind was elsewhere. "You said it's for the best and I—"

Her next words were cut off when the door swung open to reveal Doris Edwards. The woman wore a purple velour tracksuit and slippers.

"Yes?" Doris peered at them.

"Miss Doris? It's Heath Blackwood. I was hoping to have a few minutes to speak with you?"

At first the elderly woman looked confused, and he feared this was just another wild-goose chase. But he had to at least give it a shot. Beau Weatherly was right. He needed to do all he could to find answers. His personality wouldn't let him just leave it without at least trying everything he could to get to the truth.

"Blackwood?" The woman's brow wrinkled as she squinted at him. She stared for a few more moments and her brow cleared. "Of course. Why, you must be Anne's boy."

"Yes, ma'am. That's me." He gave her what he hoped was a reassuring smile.

"My word but you've grown into a fine young man. Let's have a look at you." Doris pushed her glasses higher up her nose. "Anne must be so proud."

"Well, I—"

"And who's this with you? Your missus?"

"No, this is my sister Lily."

"That's right. There were triplet girls." Doris looked at Lily, then checked the space behind them. "There must be two more just like you."

"There are three of us, but only me here tonight. And we're fraternal triplets, so not exact replicas, but we do resemble one another." Lily gave the older woman an encouraging smile.

"Well, come in, come in." Doris opened the door wider and stepped aside. "Have a seat. You're in luck, my friend from GreatStore came to visit today and brought me some cider and donuts. She remembered how much I love apple cider and cinnamon donuts in the fall. It's so wonderful that I have something to offer you."

Heath sat on the couch with Lily. He started to decline the offer of refreshments, but before he could, Lily elbowed him in the side. He shot his sister a quizzical look and mouthed, "What?"

"That would be lovely, thank you so much," Lily said as Doris scurried over to the other side of the room, where a small kitchenette was located.

"She was very excited to be able to offer us refreshments," Lily told him quietly. "She might be more willing to talk if we accept her hospitality."

"Good point," he said. Maybe having his sister along was a smart move.

As it turned out, it was. Maybe the smartest move of his life. After Doris had served them the cider and donuts, she told Heath that his mother had buried her secret.

"Her *secret*?" he asked.

Doris nodded. "She told me she buried it next to that gnarled oak tree behind the swings. She said she considered the swings her special spot with James."

Heath dropped Lily off and spoke with his other sisters. He explained he was going to see if he could dig up what Anne had buried so long ago. They offered to accompany him, but he told them he was going to ask Jade. He expected some flak for his decision, but they exchanged glances and nodded, wishing him luck with both the Jade and the dig.

He pulled out his phone on the way to his G Wagon after leaving his sisters, opening the screen to Recent Calls. He touched his thumb to the screen and called Jade. She might hang up on him or not answer when his name appeared, but he had to at least try. Doing this didn't feel right without her. *Nothing* felt right without her.

She picked up on the third ring. At least he'd gotten over that hurdle.

"Jade? I know you're angry and you have every right to feel that way, but please hear me out. You can decide what to do after that. I won't pressure you if you want nothing more to do with me."

"What do you want?" she asked after a long moment of silence.

"I'm on my way to the park."

"The park?" She sounded confused.

"I went to see Doris Edwards and—"

"Oh, Heath."

"I know. I know. But please just listen to what I found out."

"All right. I'm listening."

He jumped into the driver's seat and started the SUV. "She said my mother buried a letter in the park before she left town."

"Say what?"

"She asked Doris to tell James about the letter once

his own children were grown. Or if Anne's son ever came looking for information," he explained.

"And you believed her? Heath, you know this could be nothing but a snipe hunt, right?"

"Yeah, I know that, but I at least have to try. If it turns out it's nothing but the nonsensical ramblings of a woman with the beginnings of dementia, I'll drop the whole thing. I promise."

"You could be in for a big disappointment," she warned.

"I know but I have to check it out. And I want you there with me when I do it."

"Why me?"

"Because I can't imagine my life without you." Honesty was the best policy.

She was silent for so long, he was afraid she'd hung up. "Jade?"

"I'm here. I'm just trying to process what you just said."

"Well, I know I didn't act like it the other day, but it's true. I can't imagine being without you. Will you meet me at the park? Please."

Evidently, his please got to her because she heaved a sigh into the phone. "How about if I meet you in the park and we look for whatever this thing is? We don't have to make any decisions or plans right now."

"So you'll meet me?"

"Charlie and I are leaving right now. I'll bring a shovel. I have plenty here at the zoo."

Heath chuckled, realizing he hadn't thought about how he was going to find this note. "Thank you. I can't tell you how much this means to me."

Heath waited next to his vehicle at the park and went immediately to open Jade's door when she pulled in next to his Mercedes.

"Thank you for coming." He reached out.

She put up a hand as if to prevent him from touching. "What if there's nothing here or if there is, the answer isn't the one you want?"

"Then I will deal with it."

She shook her head, her expression sad. "That's easy to say now."

"No, it's not but I'm not going to run away from my feelings."

Her gaze searched his. "I want to believe you. I really do. But…you hurt me."

He couldn't wait any longer. Drawing her into his arms, he urgently whispered, "I'm sorry," over and over again.

He finally pulled away enough to look into her eyes. "I love you, Jade Fortune. I should have said that days ago. I'm damn sorry I didn't."

She gave him a watery smile. "I love you too, Heath."

His heart clutched at seeing that smile. It was like the sun returning after endless days of dreary clouds. He leaned down and kissed her.

Charlie woofed from the back seat of Jade's truck.

Jade used the back of her hand to wipe the tears off her cheeks. "He says he loves you too."

Heath laughed and helped the dog out of the truck. "And I love you too, Charlie. But you're going to have to get used to me kissing your mommy."

Jade went to the back of the truck and pulled out two shovels. "Where are we headed?"

"Doris said it's buried in a box on the south side of the tree."

Jade laughed. "Well, you're going to have to tell me which way is south."

Heath kissed the end of her nose and laughed as well. They went to the tree.

"Charlie, you be the lookout and let us know if you see any cops coming. I'm not sure what the law is regarding digging in the park."

Charlie barked as if he understood his job and went and sat by the tree.

"Are you sure you want to do this?" Jade asked.

Heath used one of the shovels to start digging. "I have to. Beau was right. I won't ever be able to rest until I know the truth."

"What if you don't like the answer?"

Pausing from his task, he turned toward her. "If or when that happens, I'll deal with it. How about you? If I find out that my father never wanted me, how will you feel about me then?"

"How could you think it would matter to me? I know who you are, what sort of man you are. That's all that matters to me." Locking eyes with him, she vowed softly, "I don't care about your birth story. I love the man you are today, Heath Blackwood. You backed me up when I made an outrageous claim, took me to a silly reunion to help me save face, put up with my disobedient dog, helped my friend Billy and helped me put on a wonderfully memorable Halloween for the kids of Chatelaine."

He winked at her. "Wow. I did all that?"

"Yeah. And more."

"And more?"

"You made me feel loved and desirable," she whispered.

"That's because you *are* lovable and desirable."

She gazed at him tenderly. "See? How can I not forgive you? I know how much not knowing about the circumstances of your birth affected you."

"Breaking it off with you was the worst decision of my life. I hope you can believe that," he rasped.

"I do."

"In that case, how about if we make this engagement official?" Heath asked.

"Are you serious?"

"Yes." He nodded. "I realize we haven't known one another all that long, but I know I love you, and that's not about to change. No matter what happens."

"Maybe we should stop stalling and dig this thing up."

He shook his head. "Not until you give me an answer, because no matter what happens, I want to marry you, Jade Fortune. I love you. Whatever is in here isn't going to change that. That's why I called you before I came here."

"You..." she began and then cleared her throat. "You mean that?"

"Of course I mean it. I'm sorry for the stupid things I said and the way I behaved. I'll spend the rest of my life making it up to you, I swear."

He cupped her face in his palms and sealed his promise with a kiss. After pulling his mouth from hers he rested his forehead on hers and stroked his thumb along her lower lip.

"I forgive you because I love you and want to spend my life with you too." She kissed his thumb and gently pulled away. "Okay, let's find this thing so we can start on the rest of our lives."

They continued digging, and before long, Heath's shovel hit something solid. He dropped to his knees and pulled out a plastic grocery bag. Brushing off the dirt that clung to it, he opened the bag. Moments later, he retrieved a small rectangular-shaped item surrounded by more plastic and secured with duct tape. He pulled out a pocketknife and sliced through the layers of tape. After getting rid of the tape, he unwrapped the rest of the plastic.

Underneath all the protective layers was a black lacquer box with colorful pictures of flowers decoupaged onto the top. The box was attractive, but it was obvious that whoever had decorated the box was an amateur. Had his mother decorated it some thirty years ago?

"What the...?" Heath turned it over several times.

"Wow," Jade said. "It looks like a memory box."

He frowned. "What's a memory box?"

"It's a container people use to store mementos. Keepsakes from someone or something important."

He felt a new reverence for the item he held in his hands. Would this provide more clues to who he was and what had occurred thirty years ago between his mother and father?

With a deep inhalation he opened the lid.

Inside were a jumble of items, including a floppy stuffed brown monkey with exaggerated red lips. Why would his mother have saved something like that? What meaning did it have? He held it up and turned it around. It looked like a cheap carnival toy, the kind that were offered as prizes on those midway games.

"Oh my," Jade breathed out.

"Where did all this come from? I…" his voice trailed off and his gaze met hers over the open box.

"Do you think…?" she asked in a hushed tone.

His eyes widened. "It sure looks like it."

"These are from a traveling carnival. Just like…" her voice broke off too as she stared at him.

He shook his head. "What are the odds?"

"Pretty good I'd say."

Next, he pulled out two admission tickets. That's when he spotted a strip of photos like the kind taken in those photo booths. He lifted it from the box. For a moment he just stared at the two young people smiling and mugging for the camera. His hand shook as he gazed at the pictures.

"I know this is my mother. I have to assume this was my dad." He tried to swallow, but his throat had suddenly closed up. It was as if all the emotion he was experiencing had gathered in that one spot.

Jade placed a gentle hand on his shoulder and peered down to get a closer look. "Has anyone ever seen a picture of James Perry?"

Heath shook his head. "Lily told me the other day that they've never seen a picture of him. Haley tracked down a yearbook photo of their mother through the ancestry site she belongs to. But they haven't been able to find anything for James Perry. Do you think this is him?"

"I would say so, because he looks a lot like you... maybe a bit younger in those pictures," she murmured.

"My sisters are going to want to see these."

"Yeah. This is definitely a treasure trove." Jade sucked in a breath. "Oh, look, Heath, there's writing on the back of the picture strip."

The date was approximately nine months before Heath's birth. The note read, *Memories of our one and only night.*

Lastly, he pulled out a folded piece of paper. Must be the note that Doris was referring to. Would this hold the explanation he'd been searching for?

He leaned over and placed his lips on Jade's in a gentle kiss. Pulling back, he said gruffly, "And it won't affect how I feel about you, but I've—make that *we*—have come this far, I need to read it."

He blinked as moisture gathered in his eyes.

Taking a deep breath, he unfolded the paper and read.

Dearest James,

I'm not planning to send this, but I need to write it down and bury it forever in our place. I've loved you from the moment I met you, but I know you've always considered me just a friend. I'd hoped our one night together after the carnival would change your feelings. I'll never know if it would have because you met Leanna just a few days later. That was it for you.

When I saw how in love you were, I knew I'd have to let you go. And when you eloped after just two weeks and announced she was pregnant with triplets, I kept my own secret, that I too was pregnant with your child. You have given me one of life's greatest gifts, and I want you to be happy. I don't want to come between you and your great love or future.

I'm leaving town before anyone knows I'm carrying your son so that there won't be any gossip as you embark on your new life with Leanna. One day, the truth may lead our son to you and his siblings. I hope he can forgive me. I hope you all will forgive me.

With love,
Anne

"Wow," Heath said as he read it over again and handed it to Jade.

She read it and sniffed. "So sad. Sounds like your mother loved him very much. A true love that wasn't selfish or hurtful. I'm sorry I never got to meet your mom. She sounds like a wonderful woman."

"She was. Toward the end of her life, I was frustrated that she wouldn't discuss my father. But I like to think that if the cancer hadn't taken her so quickly after the diagnosis, she might have. I'll never know, but reading this makes me believe it to be true. She didn't hate him, she loved him," he said with a touch of reverence and wonder in his tone.

"Enough to let him go and not to cause trouble for his new family or to put you in the middle," Jade said softly.

"Yeah. I suppose James wouldn't have wanted to acknowledge me if he was newly married and expecting children with his wife." That acknowledgement hurt but he'd known going into this that he might not like everything he found out.

"Maybe, but I think your mother was also looking out for you. Think about it. Even if he and his wife accepted you, you wouldn't be a part of their little family."

"Always on the outside," he mused.

"Exactly." She nodded and placed her hand on his shoulder. "Your mother was doing what she thought best for everyone, and since your father didn't even know about you, he didn't reject you."

"Even if my mother eventually changed her mind, James was deceased, so it didn't matter." He tilted his head, resting his cheek on her hand.

"I'm sure your sisters will also appreciate the story. They'll know how much their father loved their mother, thanks to Anne's letter, and they'll know that their dad was an honorable man and didn't simply abandon you or your mother. This letter shows he'd spent the night with Anne before he even met their mother."

Warmth spread across his chest. He wasn't conceived during an extra marital affair. "You're right. I'm sure they'll be as relieved by all of this as I am."

"Thank you for sharing this with me, Heath." She wound her arms around his neck.

"I wouldn't have wanted anyone else by my side... and I'm talking about forever. I want you by my side for the rest of my life and beyond." He kissed her and held her close. "Thank you."

"For what?" she asked, sounding genuinely surprised.

"For being who you are. For coming here today with

me." He blinked rapidly. "And especially for dragging me to that carnival. I wonder if they had as much fun as we did."

"She saved all the souvenirs, didn't she?"

"But she buried them," he said.

"Like I said, she was letting go. Burying the past so she could go forward into the future with you."

They picked up the box and its contents and set it on a bench. Then Heath went back and filled in the hole they'd made and tamped down the dirt.

Afterward, he followed Jade back to her place. They brought the box and its contents into the house.

"About that engagement ring you returned to me," he said once they were inside.

"You mean the fake one?"

He shook his head. "Unlike the engagement, the ring wasn't a fake."

"So, why did you give it to me?"

"I think I knew then that I wanted it to be real. In spite of my misguided belief about needing to know my past," he admitted.

She lifted a brow. "And now?"

"I realize that was a false belief."

"I would never ever hold your birth against you. No matter what we had discovered from that letter."

He reached into his pocket and pulled out the sapphire ring. "I want this engagement to be real. Will you wear this again, Jade Fortune?"

"I would be honored." She threw her arms around him.

He kissed her. Then suddenly pulled away and looked at her.

"What? Is something wrong?"

"I just thought of something."

"Whatever it is, I'm sure we can work it out. Tell me."

"Do you think Charlie will accept me as his dad?"

"What? I...you..." Rational thought was beyond her.

"I'm willing to work at it if he is."

"You can't be serious," she giggled.

"I know how much he means to you."

"But you mean the most. Surely you know that."

"I do, and don't call me Shirley."

She swatted him on the chest. "You're terrible, Heath Blackwood. Teasing me like this."

"I was only half teasing. I know Charlie is important to you."

"He is, but right now he's going to get a chew bone, and we're locking the bedroom door."

The next day, Jade accompanied Heath to his sister Lily's place. After calling her to tell her he had important news that affected all of them, all of the triplets gathered at Lily and Asa's home.

First, Heath announced his and Jade's engagement, and all three sisters flew to her and gave her a hug. They welcomed her to the family and told Heath what a lucky guy he was.

"Maybe I'm the one who's lucky," Jade said.

All three sisters laughed uproariously.

"Despite your being mean to me—" Heath said pulled out the photo strip and carefully passed it to Lily to share with the other two "—I want to share this with you."

The triplets passed the photo back and forth among themselves, tears streaming down their cheeks.

"It's the only picture we have of our dad. We couldn't find him in the yearbook where he supposedly went to high school," Lily said.

"I can't tell you what this means to us," Haley said.

Heath also shared the letter with his sisters. "I wanted you to know the story behind it all. Our father must have been a pretty special guy to have women like both our mothers love him as much as they did."

"Like father, like son," Jade whispered and took his hand in hers.

Epilogue

"That was a wonderful supper, Jade. Thanks so much for inviting us," Lily said.

Jade and Heath, who had moved out of the hotel and into Jade's spacious log home several weeks before, had invited his sisters and their loved ones to supper.

Jade smiled at them. "You're welcome, and I'm so glad you could come. I grew up in a big family, but Heath didn't, and I know he enjoys spending time with each and every one of you."

"When we're not overwhelming him, you mean," Haley added lightly.

Heath looked around the large dining table at his sisters and their families. His gaze came to rest on Jade, and his heart overflowed with gratitude. She had helped him accept the past. He couldn't change what had already happened—no one could—but he could appreciate and love the family he had going forward.

"You're probably wondering why I gathered you all here today," he said and stood up. He couldn't prevent himself from grinning at the puzzled expressions on everyone's faces. Even Jade was giving him a quizzical look. He held up his wine glass. "Man, I've always wanted to say that. Makes a guy feel important."

His sisters all groaned and rolled their eyes at him. Lily threw her napkin at him.

"I have something for each of you," he said and stacked three colorfully wrapped packages on the table.

"But it's not Christmas yet," Haley protested.

"This is just something extra. Not a Christmas gift." He passed them out. "It was something I wanted to do."

Lily opened the gift and immediately burst into tears.

Heath's stomach dropped. Had he miscalculated? "Lily, I'm so sorry. I didn't mean—"

She jumped up and ran to him. Giving him a tight hug, she said, "These are happy tears, you dope. This is perfect."

Haley and Tabitha went to him too. "Group hug," they proclaimed.

"So, you like them?" he asked when they'd released him from the hug.

"That's so thoughtful of you."

"What made you think of it?"

Lily looked to Jade, but she shook her head. "He thought of this all on his own."

"I thought you all might want a picture of our father without my mother in it," he said of the pen-and-ink drawings of James Perry he had commissioned from the photo strip. He'd had the pictures drawn, matted, and framed.

"Heath?" Jade cleared her throat. "Check out that gift for you under the tree."

Heath went to the Christmas tree they'd put up just

yesterday. Color rose in his face as he recalled what they'd done in front of the tree once they'd decorated it. There was one lone package under the tree. He brought it back to the table and began to open it.

"Great minds think alike," he said as he held up the drawing of his mother and father. The artist had obviously copied one of the pictures from the strip from the photo booth.

"Now that we know the true story of what happened, I thought you might want that memory," Jade said softly. "We'll be able to tell our children about both sides of their family tree."

He blinked back tears and went to her. He hugged and kissed her, knowing they were forging a bond that wasn't meant to be severed. Ever.

* * * * *